THE
HIGHEST
STAND

BY

TONIE CAMPBELL

www.scobre.com

Scobre Press Corporation
2255 Calle Clara
La Jolla, CA 92037

Scobre Press books may be purchased for educa-
tional, business or sales promotional use.

First Scobre edition published 2003.

Edited by Debra Ginsberg and Chris Passudetti
Copyedited by Anna Kaltenbach
Illustrated by Larry Salk
Cover Design by Michael Lynch

ISBN 0-9708992-5-4

TOUCHDOWN EDITION

www.scobre.com

CHAPTER ONE

SHOWING UP

As always, I arrived at the Olympic stadium early on race day. I didn't like to feel rushed. The officials checked my credentials at the entrance to the warm up area and let me in with a smile. The weather was perfect. The rain cleared and the day was starting to heat up. I found an area on the field to place my gear and set up my base camp for the next hour until I'd be taken into the stadium to race for the gold medal along with seven other competitors. I watched their nervous expressions and smiled fondly. As the oldest of the bunch, I felt their eyes on me, admiring my calm expression, and trying to match it.

Warm-up laps helped me focus before a big race. Some athletes hate warming up, saying it only makes them more nervous. Not me. I could talk myself right out of being nervous. Two more laps, Dede. Watch those sprinkler holes. Don't want to sprain an ankle thirty minutes before the biggest race of your life.

The grass beneath my feet was the brightest green imaginable. The problem was, I couldn't take my eyes off of it. Concentrate on your technique, Dede, I told myself. And quit looking at the ground! Okay, go through the checklist. Arms? Good, ninety degrees at the elbow, wrist relaxed, thumbs up. Legs? Hamstring's kinda tight on the left leg, spend a little more time stretching, but don't overdo it. Head? Jaw's loose, neck straight. Technique? Good. Bouncy, feeling light, paw the ground with every step. I stared back down at my feet making sure that I wasn't thumping the ground, a habit that could end any chance at a medal.

That last warm-up lap was way too quick. Now I'm feeling hot. I shouldn't have worn the sweat top under my jacket. Slow down, Dede. Remember that hamstring. Give it time to catch up to the rest of your body.

Colin Beckham, Great Britain's finest track-star, flew by and shot me a confident head nod. Don't look. Pretend you don't even see him. Too late, he saw you staring. Man, he looks good today. I guess he's all right after clipping that hurdle last round. Colin's body was designed for this race, not too tall, he was built like a sprinter and really flexible. Breaking that world record must have seemed easy for him.

I slowed down a bit. You're too hot, Dede. Walk the rest of the way. Stop here and stretch. Go slow. Follow your own routine. Today's your day.

I finished my last lap and went to get some water. Dehydration is a big problem for a runner, but I was careful not to drink too much and cramp up. Water discipline is key. I sipped from the tiny paper cup and heard a familiar voice from behind the fence that separated the athletes from everyone else. "How you feeling, Champ?" Coach Ken Matsu was watching me from the stands.

"Matsu," as all his athletes lovingly called him, had an untraditional style of coaching, mandating that his athletes get in touch with their inner self before a race. Since I met him, during my senior year in high school, he had been teaching me to find that inner self. But finding it before the biggest race of my life was a daunting task. I looked up from my stretching position. "Feeling good, Matsu," I said, hiding the fact that my left hamstring continued to scream.

"Good," he replied with a disbelieving look on his face.

The warm-up field was a small grass area only about the size of a basketball court. Coaches, fans and friends had to stay behind the chain-link fence that separated the athletes from everyone else. The area hummed with excitement. Scrambling fans pushed bits of paper through the tiny square holes in the fencing, begging for autographs from just about anyone who passed. Matsu acted as a buffer against these occasionally aggressive autograph seekers.

The seven men who stood in the way of my ultimate dream ran and stretched all around me. Celebrity-like Colin Beckham warmed up on the other side of the field and attracted a crowd that even included some of his competitors. Fellow Brit, Nigel Thorton, a good athlete himself, but mostly thought of as a spy for Colin, and Canadian, Vander Parks, huddled around Colin like children, hoping some of his talent would rub off. If they were lucky, Colin would run fast enough and gather them in his "slip stream," pulling them into medal contention. As for me, I stood alone. Mike Stone, a fellow American and my close friend off the track, didn't qualify for the medal round. This left myself and the fiery Texan, Tommy Johnston, as the only Americans in the race.

I was last to the practice hurdles and since the race organizers only gave us a few to warm up with, everyone jockeyed for position. Some tried to impress the others, taking the hurdles faster than necessary, while others took their time, as if to say, "I'm cool and ready." I tried to be one of these athletes.

As I took a few more hurdles, everything started to feel right and it showed. I felt the others begin watching me, taking mental notes. That's right, they couldn't count the old man out of the race just yet. Sure, I was thirty-one years old (ancient in track and field terms), but I didn't come here just to prove that my old legs could compete against their young ones, I came to soar past them and take home gold.

This was the third time I had been an Olympian. Some of these kids were still in grade school when I raced in Tokyo, others were college athletes when I fell short in Paris, and four years ago when I missed the Games with an ankle injury, I watched many of these boys chase down their Olympic dreams in Montreal. They knew me too and probably never expected to see me here warming up. But what they didn't know was that I'd been chasing down gold for most of my life. Yes, I'm thirty-one years old, and yes, my body has aged. But so has my mind. I've been running this race for fifteen long years and although the youthful glow in my cheeks has faded, my desire *has grown stronger.*

"Go for it Savage!" an excited fan yelled out.

I looked up to where the shout came from and waved. But instead of finding the face behind the voice, I noticed a group of four young boys sprinting back into the stadium after tracking down their objective, ice cream. Cones in hand, they scrambled for their seats. What caught my eye was the fifth boy trailing a few yards behind, calling out with ice cream dripping down his hand. The four leading boys hurried into the stadium as though he wasn't even there. I watched, feeling sorry for him in a way that only someone who had been through it could. Pictures of myself, a smallish, nerdy, twelve-year-old, quickly came to mind.

"I got Tim." Isaac Gwynn rumbled in a gruff voice. "Ike," as he was better known, or "Spike" to those he wanted to scare, stood a full four inches over the rest of the neighborhood kids waiting to hear their names called for a game of touch football.

Tim, a good athlete who was always on Ike's team, took position behind his ill-tempered captain. Tony, the other captain, knew the drill. They'd picked these teams a million times. And even though he and Ike were always captains, Tony never got first pick.

"Paul," Tony pointed with some degree of pleasure.

"Rudy," said Ike, glaring back at Tony. Paul and Rudy went to their assigned spots and Tony pretended to struggle with his next decision. He only paused trying to outthink Ike, but the end result was the same. "I'll take Joe," he finally said.

I was small, even for a twelve-year old, so when I stood tip-toed in the back of the group, I still wasn't noticeable. Even if they had noticed me though, with my thick glasses duct-taped together, and my ribs sticking out like I hadn't eaten in years, there was no chance they were going to pick me.

"Drew," Ike sighed.

"George," Tony snapped quickly.

I fidgeted in the back, as the crowd shrunk down to the final three: Edward, the new kid, and myself. The new kid hadn't been tested yet, so I felt like I'd be a pretty safe bet. In the captains' minds, however, the smelly old socks we set up as out-of-bounds markers were more welcome in the huddle than I was.

Usually, my friends Howard and Jerry attended these games with me. This made things a little easier because the three of us got picked on together. But the other day, Jerry tripped Ike by accident when he was going out for a pass. Ike got so angry that he ran over to Jerry and punched him in the stomach as hard as he could. You don't know Jerry, but he's even skinnier than I am. So when Ike's fist landed in his stomach with a smack, Jerry leaned over and puked on Ike's foot. And that's when things got even worse. Howard tried to help Jerry to his feet and Ike punched him in the head. I wished I could have stood up for my friends, but Ike was so big and strong, there was really nothing I could do.

When I saw Howard and Jerry in school the next day they said they were officially retired from backyard football. So, with my best friends (and fellow nerds), staying home, whatever abuse I was facing today, I'd be facing it alone.

I decided to show up to the game anyway, even though Howard and Jerry thought I was crazy. To tell you the truth, I was pretty scared. After all, Ike's shoes were still stained with Jerry's lunch, reminding me of how quickly the bully could snap. Plus, I knew he wasn't finished with Jerry and was frustrated that he didn't show up today. Now there was only one nerd left to pick on, me – Dede Savage. Even though I knew this, I thought that if I could just prove to everyone that I was a good football player, maybe they would leave me alone.

It was Ike's turn to pick now and with only three of us to choose from I smiled at him in a gesture of peace. "Not a chance Deidra. I'll take the new kid, and Edward, you're with them."

Great, picked last again. I kicked at a pile of dirt and took my place behind Tony.

"Our ball," Tony barked. "Huddle up," he called out and the five of us grouped together out of earshot of the other team. As always, Tony quarterbacked and called all the plays. He was a pro. "Paulie, down and out," he said, drawing the route on the palm of his hand. "I'll hit you at Mrs. Jackson's mail box." Paul nodded. "Joe, you do the same thing on the other side. Just past Mr. Washington's car." Joe nodded, clapping his hands. "George, hang back and block. If nobody's open I'll dump it to you over the middle." Tony was all business.

"I'll be there," George answered.

Tony continued, "Okay, on three. Ready…"

"Wait! What about me?" They *did* know I was on their team, didn't they?

7

George, Paul and Joe looked at me and then turned to Tony. "What about you?" Tony barked, eyeing me down.

"What do I do? Where do you want me to go?" I asked. Tony glared at me, upset that I reminded him he'd gotten stuck with me on his team. "Should I go long?" I begged Tony, envisioning myself spiking the ball in the end zone.

"No chance. Just hike me the ball and stay out of the way, Deidra."

I dutifully stood hunched over the ball as Tony surveyed the defense. With Ike right on top of me, snorting like an animal, Joe, Paul and George waited for my snap. "I'm gonna tear your head off, Deidra." I swallowed hard and braced myself. Ike then pointed at Tony over my shoulder, "You're mine and that's a fact of life, T." He taunted.

"That's your man Deidra!" Tony pointed at Ike nervously.

"Spike" stood about three inches from my face and I looked up into his reddish eyes. He was a full head taller than me and must have outweighed me by fifty pounds. Being picked last no longer bothered me; I just wanted to make it through that play with my head still attached to my body.

"No problem," I shrugged, faking confidence. Ike scoffed as Tony began the count, "down, set, hut one, hut two, hike!" I hiked the ball and before I looked up, it was over. Ike put a mean hit on me and sent me reeling backward into Tony, where the three of us collapsed in a heap on the chewed up field for a loss of six yards. When I hit the ground, Ike made sure to step on my fingers and throw his elbow into my nose. Although it was only a game of touch football, when "Spike

Gwynn" was playing, touch and tackle were the same thing.

Spike jumped up and broke into a clumsy celebration dance. When I finally regained my feet, Tony was standing. He spiked the ball sharply into the ground just inches in front of me, yelling, "you're worthless Deidra!" There was nothing I could say. Blocking Ike was an impossible assignment, but Tony didn't care. With my fingers throbbing and my newly taped glasses broken again, all I could do was take it. I started to realize that the only place I was going to catch the winning touchdown pass, or make the game saving interception, was in my sleep, because out here on the field I'd never get the chance.

The rest of that afternoon was no different. I'd get in Spike's way and he'd put me on my back. When the game finally ended, I walked home, beaten up and muddied.

On the way back to my house I closed my eyes and dreamed that I was running for a touchdown. I was flying past Joe, spinning around Tony, and barreling over Ike into the end zone. I came back to reality when I heard the honking of a bicycle horn behind me. I knew that sound anywhere, it was Ike!

Frantically, I turned around. Ike and Tony were racing toward me on their bikes. The moment I saw them, I started sprinting. I knew this routine. They would probably give me another wedgie, or worse, a black eye.

"Slow down Deidra, we just want to talk to you." Tony laughed.

"Yeah, we won't hurt you this time, we promise," Ike snarled, heaving a small stone at me. For some reason, I didn't believe him.

The houses in our neighborhood were right next to one another, so rather than staying on the street, where Ike and Tony could chase me on their bikes, I jumped over some bushes and started running through my neighbor's backyards. Tony and Ike hopped off their bikes and gave chase. I could hear their heavy breathing behind me as I climbed over short fences, ran through pricker-bushes and climbed up and over trees to escape them. After running through five or six yards, I couldn't hear them anymore. I was sure I'd outrun them.

Out of breath and out of gas I peeked around the corner – no sign of them. All I had to do now was make it across the street and I would be in my house, safe and sound. But just as I made my way around the curving sidewalk I saw them, waiting for me in front of my house. There was no place to run.

Fifteen minutes later, I was hanging from my underpants on Mr. Sloan's fence. Ike said that it was my punishment for running away from them. As the sun set behind me and my boxers slowly ripped, I wondered when I would be able to stop running and face Ike and Tony.

An hour later when Dad came home, he saw me hanging from the fence. I was a little embarrassed, but I also felt relieved. Now that Mom and Dad knew about this, those bullies would have to stop bugging me. Right?

After dinner that night Mom, Dad and I sat down for a long talk. Talks with my parents were always tough because I'm an only child. This meant that it was always two against one. Anyway, when Mom saw that my underpants had been torn into shreds she was ready to call the national guard or at the very least, Principal Juarez. I thought about this and realized that those bullies would probably torture me twice as much if she notified the school. So I asked her not to, "I can handle these guys, Mom." Just as these words came out of my mouth I wished I could have them back. How the heck could I handle these guys?

Before I could take my stupid comment back, Dad, an ex-marine who fought in the Vietnam War, concurred with me, "he's right Nancy, if you call the school, those bullies will always pick on him. Let Dede handle it himself." Dad was always an advocate of facing fears. He patted me on the back before turning on the television and ending the conversation, "you head back there tomorrow. Once they see you're not afraid of them, they'll stop picking on you."

"Who said I'm not afraid?" I forced a smile as I re-wrapped my glasses in another layer of duct-tape.

Sometimes showing up is the hardest thing to do in life. The next day I put on some new shorts and went back to the football field even though Tony had told me not to. They were choosing sides again and as I took my place in the back on my tiptoes, I watched the same teams picked in front of me one by one.

After Ike had run over me for the tenth time in a row that day, I finally gathered the courage to confront Tony in the huddle. We were losing badly and everyone was ready for some kind of change. What better opportunity for me to go out for a pass? Tony was drawing the routes on his hand and tried to assign me to block Ike again.

My heart pounded and my hands shook as I planned what

I'd say to him. "Tony," I called out.

He looked at me and I went blank, "What, Deidra?"

I swallowed hard, "Tony, you've got to give me a chance. I'm going downfield on this play, so if you want score a touchdown you know where to find me." Tony was only half listening when I started to speak, but my request grabbed his attention.

Everyone stared at him and waited for a response. Looking at me sternly, he said, "Okay, you've got one chance, but I'm only throwing you the ball if you're wide open." I couldn't believe he actually listened to me.

When I scurried to the line of scrimmage and lined up across from Tim, the fastest guy on Ike's team, I was excited. I never got to go out for a pass. Right when Tony called "hike," I bolted toward the end zone as fast as I could, shocking everyone on the field, including myself. Tim was late following me and when I looked up, I had at least fifteen yards on him. Wide open, I locked eyes with Tony, who didn't want to throw me the ball. But with Ike bearing down on him hard, and no other options, he finally heaved a prayer downfield at the last second. Ike bowled him over as he let it go, but he was too late and the ball was already spiraling toward me perfectly.

If I keep my speed I'll get it right in stride, I thought. I'd seen a hundred football games on television and knew exactly how to catch a pass. Let it drop over your shoulder and into your hands, then pull it into your chest. Here she comes, just squeeze it and score. Tony, still lying on the field beneath Ike, watched closely as I started to haul it in…only to see me come up empty-handed. The ball slipped right through my fingers, then bounced off the ground and came back up to hit me square in the mouth. I thought for sure today was my day, but before I knew what happened I was face down in the dirt with a bloody lip, staring at the dropped ball a few yards in front of me.

An instant later, Tony was screaming and pushing me, "Come on Deidra, you were wide open. Don't ever try convincing me to throw you the ball again."

I ran to the huddle, fighting back tears. I'd missed my chance.

CHAPTER TWO

STANDING UP

The only thing left to do was check the assignment sheet posted on the fence near the warm-up hurdles. Waves of energy pulsed through the warm-up area and I looked up from my stretch, as the others stopped what they were doing to begin the very deliberate walk to check lane assignments.

As far as I was concerned, the real race had already begun. This part of the experience was what I called 'the dance.' I wanted to maintain the cool and ready appearance that I'd established during warm-ups to intimidate the other runners. I finished my stretch before making my way over to the sheet, careful not to acknowledge any of my competitors, and also not to give anything away from my reaction to the lane assignments. Lane assignments can totally change the complexion of a race. I needed to know where my key competitors were going to be, in order to plan a good strategy.

With my hands on my hips and stretching backward, I

stared at the sheet. I was particularly interested in myself and Colin Beckham. Not only was he the favorite, but he was also my long time nemesis. The last time I ran in the Olympics, when I was only twenty-three years of age, Colin, three years my junior, took home the gold.

I scrolled down the names, keeping a mental tab on where everyone was assigned. There I was, Dede Savage, lane Four. I tried to hide my excitement. Stay cool, Dede. I didn't want to let the rest of the field see me celebrate, but I was excited to be running in the middle of the track. Lucky number four was traditionally considered the fast lane. Still, I wouldn't let myself lose focus. You have to run the race first, you haven't won anything yet.

Now that I had the lane assignments etched into my brain I could start to visualize how I wanted everything to unfold. I started putting the race together piece by piece in my mind. Okay, Colin drew lane three. He'll be on my left. He'll get out fast but I can't let that rattle me. I'll set my starting blocks an inch closer together, that should help my hamstring at the start. By being closer to the line, I'd put more pressure on my hands and take some off my legs. I'd get out a little slower but that was okay, I'd make it up during the race. Be careful setting up the blocks, I reminded myself. Don't forget that Colin likes to run to the right side of his lane and you always swing left. You'll crash or catch an elbow if you're not careful. That'll end your medal hopes real quickly. You've got too much riding on this to go down on a rookie mental mistake like that.

In a race regularly decided by no more than a few hun-

dredths of a second, there was no detail too small. Every little thing was critical and could mean the difference between gold and disappointment. I knew where my competitors were and I knew where I'd have to set up my blocks in order to give myself a chance at gold. My game plan was set, but that wasn't close to enough. Execution was everything. After all, a baseball scout can tell a pitcher where to throw a pitch to strike Barry Bonds out, but if that pitcher can't execute, you can wave the ball goodbye.

It was just about time to move over to the stadium, but I decided to go through a couple of full speed sprints first. I knew this was dangerous with that uncooperative hamstring, but I needed to know how well my leg would hold up. "Go!" I heard the imaginary gun go off in my head, simulating race conditions. I came out of my crouch and the muscle paused initially, but then responded and I got up to speed quickly. I could always tell how fast I was going by the noise the wind made in my ears. I heard the hurricane in my head and smiled. Looking good, I thought, slowing up carefully, knowing that most athletes hurt themselves trying to stop too quickly.

I focused on the neat geometric rows of hurdles and lane markers, trying to cool down, hoping my hamstring wouldn't tighten up. The eight of us stood in a single file line, waiting to be led out of the practice facility and onto the track. This line reminded me of grade school. I remembered waiting in line for an assembly that would change my life.

"Stay in line, boys and girls," Mrs. Loggins reminded my sixth grade class as we stood impatiently in the hallway leading into the auditorium. I was at the front of the line with Howard and Jerry right behind me. The three of us were inseparable. To the rest of the world, we looked as if we were tied together like my broken glasses. We had a lot in common and I guess that's why we stuck together. Each of us were smaller than the rest of our classmates, spectacled, and above average students. For one reason or another none of us was very popular, and nobody let us forget it. But that was okay. The three of us faced the abuse as a group. We were kind of like a team that always loses, carrying each other off the field in defeat.

In class before the assembly, Howard, Jerry and I, convinced Mrs. Loggins to bring us down early so our class could get the best seats. She reluctantly agreed. We filed into the auditorium and the three of us quickly found the best seats in the house, front row, dead center, just a few feet away from where the speaker would be standing. "I hope he took a shower today," Jerry held his nose, celebrating how close our seats were to the stage. Howard and I laughed. We were nerds and stuff like that was funny to us.

Howard tapped me on the shoulder, "hey there's your girlfriend."

I turned around and saw Carla Romero, the girl I had liked since the third grade (but never had the guts to talk to), sit down behind me. I was sure she was the prettiest girl I had ever seen. She had brown hair and the darkest eyes you could imagine. I turned away from her before she noticed me staring, "yeah, I wish," I said.

Jerry laughed, "pretty smooth look you gave her."

I started to blush and changed the subject, "let's just watch the assembly, Jerry." This was truly a perfect afternoon, no class and the three of us sitting together in front row seats. Plus, I could glance over my shoulder at Carla Romero. I just had to smile. Today was a good day. But my happiness was put on hold, when out of the corner of my eye, I spotted Ike and Tony. They were walking down the aisles slapping kids on the backs of their heads or faking a punch at them.

Without speaking a word, the three of us ducked, trying to keep Ike and Tony from spotting us from across the room. If we stayed still and quiet maybe they wouldn't notice us. Just as this thought entered my head I felt a tickle in my nose – a sneeze was coming. My nose twitched and my eyes began to close. Howard shook his head at me sadly, mouthing the word "no." Jerry spoke frantically, "hold it, Dede!" But it was too late. I sneezed the loudest sneeze of my young life and when I opened my eyes and wiped off my hands, Tony and Ike were on their way toward us. Rules were rules – find the nerds and torment them. It would take them awhile to negotiate their way through the crowd, but the ball was in motion and there was no way to stop it.

In the meantime, Principal Juarez took the stage and spoke tentatively into a humming microphone, "Find your seats, boys and girls." He gave the mike a few light taps, settling it down, and the crowd quieted. "If you'll direct your attention up here, please, I'd like to bring out our special guest speaker. About twelve years ago he was a student here, just like you boys and girls, so if you're looking for proof that you can achieve your dreams, look no further than this stage. Please welcome a local hero who just came home from winning an Olympic gold medal in team handball, Mr. Michael Anthony!"

The crowd only gave a half-hearted ovation as he took the stage, but I was already convinced. I applauded wildly. He leapt out from behind the curtains with that shiny gold medallion dancing around his neck, looking like a superhero. I stared at the gold medal intently. It was the most beautiful thing I had ever seen. The color gold is really striking. Wherever you see that color, your eyes just stick to it. So it made perfect sense to me that in life, first place was awarded gold. What other color would the winner want?

Now I don't know if it was the way it twinkled, the richness of the color, or the detailed carvings on the medal itself, but I was so completely caught up in it that I forgot about everything else around me. Michael Anthony glided across the stage in his U.S.A. sweatshirt and the auditorium seemed to disappear. It was just me and that gold medal. For a moment, I stopped thinking about being a nerd.

Just as Michael started into his speech the world came rushing back to me. Ike and Tony were bearing down on us from the end of the row. "I think your seats are in the back girls," Ike scowled, standing over Howard, who jumped up from his seat like a grasshopper, not wanting to take another punch in his head. Jerry stood up as well, clutching his stomach and trying not to look down at Ike's stained right shoe, "no problem, Ike," he said. Sadly, I started to stand up too, but before I could get too far, something came over me.

I stood there with my back to Ike and focused on Michael Anthony's words. "Now how many of you out there have a dream, raise your hands." It's like he was talking directly to me. I raised my hand. I wasn't really sure what my dream was, but I knew that I wanted to have one. I'm sure Ike was paying no attention, but Michael's words sparked something inside of me. "You need the courage to stand up to people who try and tell you what you can't do. Let them know that the only person who can say what you're capable of is you." I stopped in my tracks, turned around to face Ike and without a word, sat back down in my seat, motioning for Howard and Jerry to do the same. The road to my dream began in that moment.

I looked Ike square in the eyes and with all the guts I could muster, I told him something he'd probably never heard before in his life, "no." And I calmly turned my attention back to the stage.

"Come on, Dede," Jerry pleaded, tugging at my sleeve, "Are these seats really worth risking our lives over?"

Tony chimed in, "yeah, Deidra, listen to your little friend, he's got a point."

Ike growled, visibly confused, "you must be crazy, trying to…" But before he could finish I cut him off, this time with more resolve in my voice, "no, Ike."

My courage must have been contagious. Howard sat back down, crossing his arms in defiance of Ike. A moment later Jerry also dug in his heels, plopping himself back into his chair. The speaker continued, "In order to reach your dream, you have to stand your ground. When your critics say you're crazy for thinking you can do it, well you have to look them straight in the eye and tell them that you are in control of your destiny and no one else."

I stared at Michael Anthony, his gold medal twinkling in the fluorescent lights of our middle school auditorium, and I wasn't scared anymore. Still, the bully continued, "I'm giving you one more chance, Dede, and then there's going to be trouble." Ike raised his eyebrows expectantly, but I wasn't budging. "If you hurry up, you can still find a seat in the back without getting a fist shaped hole in your head," he pleaded. Now on any other day, this would have been enough to bring me to tears, but today it barely fazed me.

I stood up, and with Ike towering over my smallish frame I gave him a stern look and spoke, "get lost, Ike. I'm trying to hear the speaker and you're annoying me. We're not moving and there's nothing you can do about it."

It seemed like the whole auditorium heard this exchange, and for a moment everyone looked to see what the commotion was. I could see Ike shrinking under the pressure, trying to maintain his tough guy persona. He stammered for a moment, then clumsily sputtered to Tony, "Come on, this guy's boring anyway." The two bullies made the long walk to the back of the auditorium, growing smaller with each step they took away from us. Howard, Jerry and I, sat proudly in the front of the room.

Howard looked at me, shocked, as Michael Anthony finished his speech, "Who the heck are you and what did you do with Dede?"

Sitting there in the twilight of my great moment, I came to an important realization. After listening to Michael Anthony's speech, I realized that a dream of mine really could come true. I guess I was always too concerned with making it through the day without any trouble from the cool kids to think about that kind of stuff. In an instant, all of that had changed. The image of that perfect gold medal danced around in my head. I was more determined than ever to achieve my dream.

But what <u>was</u> my dream?

A pat came over my shoulder, awakening me from my trance. Carla Romero leaned over from the row behind us. "That was cool, how you stood up to Ike like that. Real cool."

I turned bright red and thanked her. Although I had just stood up to the meanest bully in school, there was only one thing I could think about. Carla Romero just touched my shoulder – now that was cool.

CHAPTER THREE

STUMBLING

The nervous official stopped us short of the entrance, hurrying ahead to make sure they were ready for us to enter. It must have been this poor guy's first big race because in his haste to make everything perfect, he'd brought us down a few minutes early. Looking down at his pocket watch he shook his head and raced back, stumbling over himself to bring us the news. None of us were pleased, knowing that a delay like this was a perfect opportunity to lose focus, or worse, for muscles to tighten up. Still, I think we all understood. It was a big race and he wanted everything to go smoothly.

As a pack, we moved down to the temporary track beneath the stadium, set up to allow for delays like this one. This was a tricky situation and I had to struggle with competing instincts in my head. I knew the younger athletes would want to rush down and get extra warm-up time in before the race, thinking this delay would give them the extra time they needed to get even more prepared. It's hard not to think this way because it only makes sense that the more warm-up time and practice you get, the more prepared you'll be. As a veteran and an old pro, I knew better.

Just as I thought, all the younger kids in the field took to the temporary track in a frenzy, trying to squeeze in extra sprints and more hurdles. They didn't realize it yet, but they were giving up gold with every inexperienced leap, stride and step they took. I don't think it's the fatigue that inevitably sets in from these frantic warm-ups, but the lack of trust you show in your own ready routine that really hurts.

I found a quiet spot on the track, and going over my strategy, tried to stay loose with quick bursts of speed followed by plenty of stretching and rest. I wanted to stay on the same level I was when we got to the stadium, no warmer or cooler than before the delay. I knew my pre-race routine worked for me and I wasn't about to mess around with what got me here.

In my twelve-year career as a professional hurdler, I'd been through many delays like this. The longest was a four-hour power outage in Tokyo, where I saw one athlete actually close his eyes and take a nap. In a competition in Los Angeles, our race was stalled for twenty minutes due to a dark rain cloud that eventually passed over us. Another time in Rome, a freak hailstorm delayed our race for close to two hours. So I'd been here before, and it was my hope that this delay would provide me with an advantage. Once again I was relying on my experience to make up for a pair of aging legs.

In between sets, I couldn't help notice what my competition was up to. Colin never looked more comfortable. Quick *bursts then stretching and rest. He was cool and ready. Those younger guys could learn a lot from watching him. Tommy Johnston, the other American and Boris Krazets, from Russia, kept a close eye on Colin and tried to keep loose in much the same way. They too could be dangerous once the race began.*

The official approached us with a solitary bead of sweat flowing down his forehead. "Okay, now it's time, gentleman," he alerted us with a head nod.

"Here we go," I thought, stumbling as I stretched one final time by grabbing my toes while keeping my knees from bending.

I stood up from my stretch, pretending not to care whether or not I was picked. "Savage," Mat said, calling me to the middle of the parking lot basketball court during our second period gym class. I breathed a sigh of relief under my breath.

I walked my lanky fourteen-year-old frame over to Mat Richards (the coolest kid in school), and stood behind him. I had grown a full six inches in the past two years and stood just a shade under six feet tall. This really made a difference for me in sports, especially basketball. Although being a team captain was still beyond my reach, I could pretty much count on being one of the first picks.

Eighth grade was shaping up to be a pretty great year for me so far. It'd been two years since my run in with Ike in the auditorium and things had really changed for me. It was like the popularity he lost by getting shown up by a nerdy sixth grader was thrust upon me. Popularity wasn't something I dreamed of or even wanted that badly, it was something that just kind of happened to me. Suddenly, I was invited to every party. All the cute girls would talk to me in class and some even called my house. I'd replaced my thick glasses with a pair of contact lenses, gained twenty pounds and grew a full head in height. I was no longer picked on because I was no longer an easy target. After all, I was bigger than many of my classmates now.

I had all kinds of new friends too. Pam Simpson, the beautiful captain of the cheerleading team, chose me to be her lab partner in science class. Mike Torelli saved me a seat everyday at the cool table in the cafeteria and Nick McCain always made sure that he and I shared the back seat of the bus on our rides to and from school. Two years earlier, I'd never even seen the back seat, let alone sat in it.

But having all these new friends made things difficult when it came to my old friends, Howard and Jerry. Unfortunately, things had changed very little for them after the three of us went head to head with the school bully. They were just as much a part of it as I was, but nobody paid attention to that, and I guess they got lost in my wake as I sprinted past them on my way to join the cool kids. We stopped going to the movies every Friday night. There were no more long talks about baseball or space travel or girls. In fact, by the beginning of eighth grade, we barely spoke at all. They still had glasses hanging from their noses and each of them had failed to hit a growth spurt like mine. They sat with the foreign exchange students at lunch, staring across at the cool table, pretending not to hope that I'd save them seats. And in my cowardice, I never did. I didn't want to be a nerd anymore, and in my eyes, all Howard and

Jerry did was remind me of the Dede Savage I wanted so desperately to forget. The one who was always the butt of jokes, the one who got so many wedgies that Mom had to buy my boxers in bulk, the one who girls never talked to, the one who was always picked last, and the one who was afraid of everything and everyone. That nerd no longer existed. The new Dede Savage was cool.

So I couldn't save my old friends seats, talk to them in the hallways or even look at them for that matter. I didn't want anyone to know that I still cared about Howard and Jerry.

Second period was an awful time to have gym at our school. The winter mornings were so cold that the frosted grass crunched beneath our sneakers as we took the field for roll call. Gym class was always tough on Howard and Jerry. And their lack of athleticism was never more on display than during pick-up basketball games we played, where the two of them were always last picked and rarely allowed anywhere near the ball.

It was an exceptionally cold day in February and Howard and Jerry stood alone in shorts as the last two waiting to be picked for the game. Mat was smiling in a pair of warm sweatpants, with the three players he'd already chosen standing behind him, anticipating his final pick. I was one of these guys. Mat put his arm on my shoulder, pointing at Howard and Jerry. "Hey Dede, should we even pick these guys or should we just play four on four?"

He asked me this question in front of everyone, including Howard and Jerry. The two worlds I was a part of collided at that moment and I knew I would need to decide which one I belonged to. I was torn, but a decision still had to be made. No matter how much I told Mat that he was the captain and choosing was his job, he relentlessly baited me to answer his question. I remembered so many times in my life that I'd wished that I could be the one doing the picking. But now that my chance had arrived, staring at Howard and Jerry, I was frozen. It should have been a moment of triumph for the three of us, but it became clear to me that I was a different person, and we were no longer on the same team.

"Look at their knees," one kid shouted from behind Mat and me. All the boys broke out laughing. Both Jerry and Howard's skinny knees chattered from the cold and they held their hands close to their chest, struggling to squeeze out any warmth they could. I knew the longer I took to make a decision, the more abuse the two of them would have to take. Still, I didn't make a move. Nobody really noticed how long I was taking and I don't think anyone cared if we ever got to the basketball game at all. Making fun of Howard and Jerry was enough of a game to keep most of them occupied for the whole period. And as much as I knew that this whole thing was going on because I wouldn't make a decision, I didn't do one thing to stop it. Howard and Jerry both stared sadly at me. Each time our eyes met, I quickly looked away. I didn't know what to do so I sat idly as the growing crowd tore into them.

Mat knew what a struggle this was for me, and seemed to enjoy my torment. He wanted me to choose once and for all which group I wanted to belong to. "So, what do you think, Dede, should we take one of your buddies or what?" All eyes were on me.

I looked at Howard and Jerry and then back at Mat and the crowd of people watching. I wanted to stand up to Mat, pick one of the guys and invite them to Stephanie Jackson's party tomorrow night too. I wanted everyone to see how great my old pals were. But I couldn't do it. Somewhere along the way I'd become a coward. I spoke loud so everyone could hear me, "Those losers aren't my buddies. They just get in the way – we're better off playing without them."

After making this comment, I walked up to Jerry, avoiding his eyes. My hand touched his chest and I pushed his skinny body directly into Howard, causing them both to crash to the ground. They tumbled over one another and the gathered crowd erupted like fans cheering uncontrollably for a buzzer-beater shot. Mat ran toward me laughing hysterically and gave me a high five.

With Howard and Jerry taken care of, the crowd quickly dispersed and we tried to get the game started. I ran past them, and shot a quick glance in their direction as I took my position on defense. Jerry helped Howard off the ground and looked back at me, shaking his head. The two of them dragged themselves off the court and went back inside. My heart sank and I remembered all the good times we used to have together. I thought about Howard's obsession with his baseball card collection and the way Jerry used to sing along to all the songs on the radio. I could hear him singing inside my head at that moment and I suddenly felt like I was going to cry. It was hard, but I held back my tears and dribbled up the court.

After class, I walked out of the gym alone. I couldn't get my mind off the way Howard and Jerry looked at me from the pavement after I knocked them over. I could see them clearly every time I closed my eyes. Howard was lying flat on his stomach and Jerry lay crumpled in a twisted ball. They winced in pain and their eyes burned holes through me. Howard's knee was scraped and Jerry's shirt was torn. Their faces were chapped with the cold and their pupils were filled with tears.

I felt terrible and walked through the halls like a zombie. What kind of person had I become? Just as this thought entered my head I crashed right into someone. A pile of books and papers flew everywhere. In a daze, I bent over to pick them up.

Oh no, I thought, looking up at who I almost rolled right over. It was Carla Romero. Now although I was now a part of the cool crowd, I still hadn't really spoken much to Carla besides the two or three words we shared in the auditorium two years ago. I wasn't shy in front of most girls anymore, but Carla was different. She wasn't impressed by my popularity. Carla stood on the outskirts of the cool crowd, and although she was always invited to parties, she did her own thing. Some of her friends were nerds, some were jocks, some were a few years older than us and some a few years younger too.

Normally I'd never have the nerve to talk to her, but I'd noticed her watching me on the basketball court the period before. I felt confident that my game winning jump-shot had impressed her. Searching for words I finally sputtered out, "Hi, Carla."

I thought I saw her give me a smile, but maybe that was how she always looked. All I know is that I started to tell her who

I was when she cut me off, saying, "I know who you are, Dede. And I wanted to talk to you."

Great, I thought.

She continued, "I noticed you on the basketball court and I saw what you and your friends did to those two boys," her calm expression turned to anger. "I used to think that maybe you were someone special – boy was I wrong. You're just like that idiot Ike who used to pick on you. How could you do that to them? I thought Howard and Jerry were your friends."

I tried to say something in my defense, but there was nothing I could say. Carla had seen me in my worst moment. Before I opened my mouth to defend myself, she started in on me again, "You're not a nice person, Dede – and that's too bad because I would have liked to get to know you better. But at least now I know the truth and I won't have to waste any more time on you." And with that she turned and walked away.

I stood in silent confusion as the late bell rang and the hallway quickly cleared. I couldn't believe what had just happened. I was bigger and stronger and cooler than I'd ever been in my life. And the only girl I'd ever liked, wanted to get to know me better. But the weird thing was that she wanted to get to know the nerd that I was, not the cool guy that I'd become.

Then I heard Jerry singing again in my head. I pictured Howard and I jumping off his diving board to see who could make the biggest splash. What had I done to my friends? I'd jumped over so many hurdles on my way to the cool crowd, but as I watched Carla disappear down the hallway, I knew that I'd definitely just stumbled over one.

CHAPTER FOUR

OUT OF THE DARKNESS

With the exception of a barely noticeable rumbling sound, the tunnel that led into the stadium was silent. We were well sheltered from the noise of the monstrous crowd in the maze-like belly, but the rumble made me pretty sure things would be different once we stepped out onto the track. From what I understood, this stadium was among the largest ever built, certainly larger than anything I'd ever run in.

They had us positioned about twenty feet from the mouth of the tunnel. Staring out into the wide-open arena from the darkness, I tried to make out the outline of the track. But looking into the blinding light of the arena with my eyes adjusted to the dark interior, I couldn't see anything but a white wall of light at the tunnel's end.

"Time to move, gentlemen," the official called. With that, eight men took a deep breath and began the methodical

walk into the stadium.

Entering a stadium illuminated for a night event is awesome. The first few seconds of blindness while your eyes adjust makes the one-hundred-and-fifty-thousand headed screaming monster coiled in the stands even more shocking as it comes into view. It takes a few more seconds before you can actually hear them, but when you do, all at once, you'd swear that a bulldozer could drive into a dynamite factory right there in the middle of the track and nobody would even notice. And this is before the race even begins.

As I entered the light for my last race I wanted the walk to seem different, but it didn't. One foot touched the ground after another, a long stare at the crowd was followed by a moment of dizziness, my arm waved at no one in particular, I heard three- hundred-thousand hands clapping, and the thunderous beating of my heart echoed throughout the packed stadium. Shielding my eyes, I tried to remain as cool as possible, not letting myself be dwarfed by the moment. I walked proudly out into the arena alongside my competitors as the ground I would eventually be running on shook beneath me.

I've walked this walk before, and no, it never really changes. With my eyes closed I stretched my arms over my head and breathed in deep through my nose, trying to draw in as much of the experience as possible. I knew that I would never walk this walk again. I could have stood there for hours and basked in the atmosphere, but I snapped out of it after a few wonderful moments. Just like that, a switch flipped in my head and from that point on I was all business. My focus was entirely directed toward the task at hand. I came to win a gold medal and behind me I could feel the drive of that dream. Years and years had been devoted to accomplishing this one goal. I quickly got to work.

I flipped my sweats decisively to the young girl positioned at the front of my lane holding a laundry basket. I was locked in and had to focus on getting my starting blocks positioned just right. I adjusted the blocks to my lean, six-foot two-inch frame, spreading the push-off pedals far apart. People said that my stance resembled a person in a running position leaned over to touch the ground. I picked this up from Matsu, who always believed in trying to stay as close to the running position as possible. It seemed to work, and though I wasn't the fastest out of the blocks, I always got up to top speed quickly.

Stepping into the blocks, it was time to take some practice starts. Countdown to race time was set at three minutes. Let's show these boys what we got, Dede, go full speed over the first three, I thought to myself. Even though these were only practice runs my feet were set in the blocks with one thing in mind, the perfect start.

Head down, quick arms, fast feet. Head down, quick arms, fast feet, I repeated in my head over and over, rising slowly to my set position. Hold. One second, two seconds, three – pow! The imaginary gun went off in my head. Now! One, two, three, four, five! I exploded off the line and accelerated hard to the first hurdle. Look up now! The first hurdle rushed toward me. Attack! Snap down, accelerate! One, two, three, attack! Again! Relax. I thought frantically and slowed to a stop. Feeling good. One more and I'll be ready.

I walked back to the line on the infield grass, analyzing

my practice run and calculating any adjustments I needed to make. Satisfied, I decided to stick with what I had and felt good going into my second practice start. Everything was set. I couldn't have been more confident.

I tore blindly through another warm-up set and was so pleased with myself that I lost focus for a moment and slowed up too quickly. And that's when I felt it. Right in the back of my thigh, the familiar burning I thought I'd worked out earlier. I knew exactly what it was. My hamstring hadn't felt right all day and I went around showboating on it like some rookie. I was furious with myself for being so careless and hoped the muscle would still respond come race time. I couldn't believe how stupid I'd been, but I'd made the mistake and now I would have to deal with it.

Seeing Carla in the hallways helped remind me of the mistake I'd made with Howard and Jerry. They were the best friends I'd ever had and I'd discarded them. The question now was, how was I going to deal with it. The rest of the school year passed without a word spoken between my two old pals and I. There weren't any more incidents like the one on the basketball court that day, but there seemed to be no way to fix what I'd broken.

Still, I wouldn't stop trying. I saved a seat for Howard and Jerry at lunch a few times, but they wouldn't sit in it. I'd ask them to go to the movies almost every Friday, but they'd usually just walk past and ignore me. In gym basketball games, I made sure to pass them the ball. I wrote about ten apology notes, maybe twenty. But nothing I did mattered to them. They continued to ignore me. And when I tried to talk to Carla, (which was every chance I got), she would usually respond with quick answers to my questions and would rarely stick around long. The good news was that she noticed me trying to make up for my mistakes. When I saved a seat at lunch for Jerry one day Carla walked past me smiling, "that was nice," she whispered.

My efforts with Howard and Jerry continued with no real results and Carla continued to speak to me only in short spurts. Until, that is, the spring of the next year, when my luck seemed to change.

There hadn't been a dance at our school in over a year due to a flood that ruined the wooden floors in the auditorium the previous fall. With the floor finally dried up, our spring dance would be held as scheduled. I knew for sure Carla was going to be there and I wanted to figure out a way to spend some time with her, or at least get her to talk to me. I called Howard and Jerry to ask them if they were coming to the dance, but neither of them would pick up the phone.

Maybe I'd never get my friends back, but I wasn't going to stop trying. I went to the dance alone and when I stood at the closed doors to the gym, hearing the muffled music pour out from a small space in-between the heavy wooden doors, I was really nervous. I put my hand over my mouth and breathed out heavily into it, checking to make sure all the chips I ate before the dance weren't still on my breath. Then, slowly, I slid into the gym.

My first objective was to find Mat. I wasn't sure exactly how to go about talking to Carla, but I was pretty sure that wandering the dance alone all night and looking pathetically friendless wasn't the right answer. After making two or three circuits around the dance floor I spotted Mat from across the room at the refreshment table and made my way over. He knew I had a crush on Carla and loved to tease me about it, constantly reminding me that I had as much of a chance of getting a date with her as I did of walking on the moon. If I wasn't so sure that Mat was my friend, I would've thought he was pretty mean sometimes.

"What's up, Mat?" I said, drawing nearer. He was talking to some of his other friends and shot me half a nod with his head. Allen, who'd never really liked me, moved over, positioning himself cleverly between Mat and I. He tolerated me being part of Mat's group, but made it very clear that I wasn't part of his. That was fine with me. Allen always reminded me of a smooth and sophisticated version of Ike anyway. He was a bully all right, but he'd terrorize with subtle gestures rather than fists, like not inviting me to a party or choosing a bench at lunch that had enough seats for everyone but me.

"Hey, what's up, Romeo?" Mat teased, finally acknowledging me.

I blushed and shrugged my shoulders. "Not much, I guess," I mumbled, embarrassed in front of Mat's other group of friends.

"Did you see Juliet?" Mat asked with a smile, obviously playing it up for Allen and his group. Now Mat knew that when it came to girls in general, and Carla in particular, I was about as subtle and graceful as a bag of hammers, so I really hated him teasing me like that in front of all these people.

Growing tired of standing around the drink table, Allen went off to the dance floor (thank goodness). The night was passing quickly and I hadn't even seen Carla yet, let alone talked to her. I was growing restless when Mat tried to reassure me. "Don't worry. She's bound to come this way. Maybe this'll be your lucky night."

I beamed with joy at the thought. "Yeah, maybe," I perked up, but Mat just burst out laughing, slapping me on the shoulder, "dream on!" he managed to sputter out, still giggling.

Mat was really starting to bother me. Was he really my friend or did he just like making fun of me? The answer was becoming more and more obvious to me and I decided to leave him at the drink table. But just before I took my first step away from him a voice interrupted, "Excuse me, I'd like to order a drink please." We both froze. I'd waited all night to hear that sound and even before she finished her sentence I knew it was Carla. Not knowing how to react, I started sweating like an animal, but Mat stayed cool and slowly turned around to face her.

"I'm sorry, did you say something to me?" Mat said.

"To us." I added bravely. Mat glared at me.

"You're in our way and we'd like to get something to drink, if you don't mind." Carla snapped at Mat, moving him aside with her hand. She never liked him and wasn't shy about it. Mat walked away, feeling little in front of Carla. I didn't follow him.

My heart started to pound as I stood alone at the drink table, just a few feet from Carla. I started to speak under my breath, "Go ahead, ask her to dance Dede."

And with that Carla turned to me, "Did you say something?" she glared.

Mat turned back, his eyes as big as saucers, excited to see me get embarrassed.

"No, I - I was talking to myself," I said shyly.

"Oh," Carla sounded disappointed and turned back to the counter. I chickened out and Mat looked over at me laughing. I really didn't want to hear it from him later, and Carla seemed like she might actually want to talk to me, so I just came out with it. "No wait," I said. She quickly turned back toward me. I continued sputtering out half-sentences, "What I meant to say was, yes I was talking to you." Her dark eyes narrowed. "I mean…what I meant to say was…" I'd gone too far, there was no turning back now. As I finally came out with it, a strange sense of comfort came over me and it actually seemed easy once I stopped being so nervous. "Would you like to dance?" I finished my sentence, managing to sound relatively confident.

It was going better than I could have imagined, and there was a chance she might even dance with me, but as the invitation was pouring out of my mouth, I failed to notice the liquid in my glass pouring out as well. A full cup of red punch splattered onto her shiny white dress. I was so caught up in the moment that I completely forgot about the drink I'd been nursing for the last half-hour. Now, with an empty cup in hand, and staring at an island shaped dark red stain on Carla's dress, I knew my luck had run out.

Before I realized I was asking her to dance, she was covered in fruit punch. She snorted her disgust at my clumsiness and stormed off to the bathroom with her friends in trail. How quickly it all fell apart. Mat stood a few feet away laughing hysterically and making me feel much worse. "That was the funniest thing I've ever seen in my life, Dede. You spilled a whole glass of punch right on her." Mat extended his hand for me to slap five with him, but I pointedly ignored him, making my way toward the boy's bathroom. I was beginning to wish I hadn't come.

Unfortunately it was almost two hours until my mother was set to pick me up and I didn't want to go through the hassle of explaining to her why I needed to come home early. I knew she and Dad would sit me down for another long talk and Dad would probably make me come back to the dance anyway. Quitting wasn't an option in the Savage house. So I decided to ride the rest of the night out.

About thirty minutes later I wandered upstairs, not paying attention to where I was going. At the end of the empty hallway I saw what looked like a crumpled up ball of white fabric sitting on a bench outside of the girls bathroom. When I got closer, I could tell it was Carla, and though she wasn't crying, I knew that she had been earlier. Her face was all red and her makeup was smudged. I thought I'd be nervous sitting by her, but I wasn't. I'd already blown my chance. All that was left to do now was apologize and say goodnight.

I sat next to her and a few moments passed before either of us said anything. Finally I blurted out, "I'm sorry about your dress, Carla. I just like you so much and you look so pretty tonight and I just get so nervous around you that I can't even think straight. I didn't mean to ruin the dance for you. I'm sorry." That was the most I had ever said to Carla at once. I finished my speech with one more, "I'm so sorry," and I got up to leave.

But she grabbed my hand before I could go, "Dede wait, will you sit with me for a minute?" I sat down quickly. "It's just so hard," she said, "there's so much pressure for everything to be perfect at these stupid things. I don't know why we can't just come here and have a good time. You know, I'm actually kind of glad you dumped your drink all over me."

I saw an opportunity to lighten the mood, "Well, anything I can do to help," I said smiling. I was starting to realize that when I didn't try so hard to impress her and just talked to her, I was a pretty likeable guy. So we talked and laughed for a while about how nervous we both were coming into the dance. I told her that I was upset about what a jerk I'd been to Howard and Jerry and she tried to help me come up with a plan to earn their friendship back. After about an hour of talking, we decided to head back downstairs before the dance was over.

We entered the gym, her with the dark red stain on her dress, and me disheveled from wandering the halls half the night. Just as we made our way through the doors, Mat and his friends came busting through, Allen close by his side, cheering and celebrating. They passed by quickly, though Mat and Allen made sure to shoot me a quick sarcastic look, obviously trying to remind me of my fruit-punch mistake earlier that night. They stampeded out the front door into the parking lot where I could see Mat's mom waiting to pick them up.

"What are they so happy about?" I asked another student on his way out of the dance.

"Principal Macon gave away a trip to the amusement park tomorrow for one student and five friends."

As it turned out, Mat was the lucky one to win that prize

and when he was picking which of his friends he wanted to take with him, I guess he forgot to include me. I turned to Carla and mumbled, trying to save some dignity and hide how much it bothered me, "That's all right, I've got lots of homework to do tomorrow anyway," but she didn't buy it and I don't think I did either. We stood there for a moment as people poured out of the gym and filed past us into the parking lot.

Turning to me, Carla asked, "so, how does it feel?"

"How does what feel?" I came back, not realizing what she was driving at.

She looked at me sideways, amazed that I could have so quickly forgotten about the way I treated my old pals. "How does it feel to have your best friend turn his back on you like you did to Howard and Jerry?"

"Terrible," I said meekly, finally understanding her point. Carla nodded as she started toward the school's main entrance, both of us realizing that the dance had ended about ten minutes ago.

I walked her outside and we looked for her friend Brenda, whose mother was supposed to be Carla's ride home. Carla was nervous because she thought Brenda may have forgotten she was taking her home. We looked everywhere for Brenda's mom's red truck. Finally, Carla spotted it, but it was rolling toward the exit two football fields away. "Oh no, they're leaving without me!" Carla shouted, overcome by panic.

I stared at the truck and then back at Carla. I looked at the two hundred yards of bushes and people and parking lot and cars ahead of me and my heart started racing. Sometimes there is a moment in life when you have to do something. You don't necessarily know why, but you have to act. A terrible night for Carla was about to get much worse. I looked over at her as she helplessly tried to wave down the truck that was pulling away. Tears came to her eyes again. And something came over me like it never had in my entire life.

Adrenaline shot through my body in a surge and I started in a full sprint toward the truck without saying a word. I jumped over bushes, tearing my pants at the seams. Then I hurdled a short fence, clearing it by two full feet. Finally I flew past exiting students like I was running on rocket fuel.

Carla shouted, "Dede wait, you'll never catch her!" But her scream was aimed at my back – I was off and running, in a dead sprint toward the truck that was quickly driving away. The truck reached the exit to the school just as I hit top speed. I wasn't slowing and was actually gaining on them as they drove slowly down the road. About ten seconds later, I shot out of the darkness and was running alongside the moving vehicle, keeping pace with it as it moved through traffic. Finally, Brenda rolled down her window to see what was going on, "Dede?" She looked confused.

I was out of breath, running as fast as I could alongside her, "Carla, you forgot Carla," I gasped, pointing back to the curb in front of the school. The truck quickly slammed on the brakes and I stopped running, huffing and puffing with exhaustion.

Brenda looked at me perplexed, "Jeez Dede, you're really fast." I stood hunched over, staring at the distance I had just covered in such a short time. I'd never really given it much thought, but yeah, I was pretty fast.

I jumped into the back seat of the truck and we turned back to pick up Carla, who was smiling and waving in the distance. I waved back from the half-opened window as we pulled around to the curb. I got out and Carla got in. "You're my hero, Dede," she said half-jokingly and half-serious.

Just before she closed the door I kissed her on the lips. I never thought I would have had the guts to kiss a girl, especially not Carla. But when I did, she smiled and I felt like I'd won the lottery.

CHAPTER FIVE

TAMING THE FIRST HURDLE

I stood in the middle of the arena floor with a foolishly strained hamstring. If it didn't cooperate this race would be over for me with the first step out of the blocks. Gripping at the back of my leg, I was sure the rest of my competitors knew what kind of trouble I was in. The damage had been done, though, and soon enough I would know whether I'd pull up lame. In the meantime, worrying about it would only take me out of my game. So I made the necessary mental adjustments, reminding myself to be aware of the strained muscle.

It was getting nearer to start time and the television camera panned across the line of athletes as we were introduced to the crowd. A few of the younger guys took this opportunity to show off a little for the audience at home, flexing their biceps or doing some quick hops. Others sent a "shout out" to a loved one watching, "hi Mom" was always popular. I could do without all this, but realizing it was part of the package of running in such an important race, I forced a polite smile into the camera and tried to maintain focus.

Through a small speaker behind us came the starter's tinny voice, "Gentlemen, take your marks," he commanded. A much more serious mood came over the starting area. Ten hurdles and a football field distance, the first to the finish line would earn gold. Eight warriors backed into their starting blocks. I followed the same routine I had for years. My right leg, the strongest, went in first. I carefully set up just as I always had, but this time mindful of that pesky left hamstring. I placed my foot onto the pedal, making sure the top two spikes of my shoes dug firmly into the track. I could have had my entire foot on the pedal, many athletes did, but I liked the feeling of having only a small part in contact with the track.

Going down the checklist in my head I knew exactly what I had to do. With my right leg feeling good and set against the pedal, the focus shifted to my hands. From my fingertips right through to my elbows everything had to be in exactly the right position or the whole thing would be thrown off. My fingers felt strong beneath the weight of more than half my body as I proceeded along. I made sure each individual part of my body was properly aligned. With everything in order I'd explode off the line, all those individual parts would come together for one perfect start.

I arrived at the last item on the checklist, the one I'd been dreading since the starter called us to our marks. I hadn't felt anything out of the ordinary in my left hamstring since the practice run, but then, I hadn't really tested it either. So there was still some uncertainty as I gingerly backed it in. The left leg was the last leg in and the first one out. Between the two, it's the hardest worked in the race. Unfortunately it was also the one that was sore. I tried to avoid cursing myself for my mental lapse during that last practice run – any negativity would slow me down at this point.

The line judge, the official in charge of making sure everyone's hands are behind the starting line, quickly ran from lane one to eight and proclaimed that everyone was ready. The starter's tinny detached voice again came over the speaker, "runners set," and I felt the rest of the field rise quickly though I didn't turn my head to look. This is where I would take my edge. I took my time and paused until I could feel that the starter's full attention was on me. Only then did I rise into the set position. I wanted him to focus directly on me so that he would fire his gun when I was ready. This would give me a slight edge out of the gates, and also help me to avoid a false start. You'd be surprised by some of the weird stuff runners will do to get the starter's attention, like yelling or humming loudly. My trick was waiting a second or two longer than the rest of the field to rise. Nothing fancy, just long enough to make sure that he was focused on me when he turned us loose.

The crowd of thousands sat quietly, awaiting the starting gun. It was only three and a half seconds from the set position to the gun. But there on the line, with my fingers strained under the intense weight of my body and sweat dripping irregularly from my forehead, it seemed like that gun would never go off.

I closed my eyes knowing the next time I opened them I

would be accelerating from a stand still to nearly twenty-five miles-per-hour toward a wooden barricade. Closing your eyes can be dangerous for some athletes, as the natural reaction when you open them is to slow down while your eyes adjust to the light. Matsu and I had trained my body to overcome this. In order to achieve that elusive perfect start we had to eliminate everything but the most essential senses. I knew exactly what was in front of me, I didn't need my eyes.

My thoughts were singular as I waited in my set. First step is seven inches from the line, an inch short and you'll have to reach for the first hurdle, an inch long and you'll crash into it. The slightest error in the beginning becomes magnified as the race wears on. If I missed my mark on that first step I would have to spend the rest of the race adjusting just to avoid a crash.

Suddenly, eight tense bodies uncoiled, exploding off the line in an automatic reaction to the first audible noise. We all heard it and reacted instinctively. My arms pumped and my legs powered out of the blocks. I was already three steps into my gold medal race when the second gunshot rang out. The crowd let out a collective gasp of disappointment, recognizing the signal for a false start. This meant that someone had began running before the gun sounded. I slowed up, gently this time, glad it wasn't me who had jumped too early. Olympic rules allow only two false starts before disqualification. Whoever just jumped, probably gave up gold in doing so. Now he would have to exhibit extra caution on the restart and most likely fall behind the pack.

The summer before my freshman year of high school was a confusing time for me. I didn't really know where I fit in. After my falling out with Mat at the dance, I found myself on the outskirts of the popular crowd. This was fine by me, except that I was no longer accepted in the nerdy crowd either. So I was kind of on my own that year. Not to mention that my great kiss with Carla didn't amount to very much. I mean, we became friends, but Carla (and especially Carla's parents), wouldn't allow anything more than that. In her house, the rule was absolutely no boyfriends until your sixteenth birthday. So Carla and I talked on the phone, went to the movies a few times (with Mr. and Mrs. Romero), and sat near one another at lunch.

She talked to Howard and Jerry for me once or twice, but even her charm didn't work on the two of them. They simply weren't ready to forgive me. It had been over a year now since the basketball incident and I just couldn't figure out a way to mend our friendship and make up for the way I treated them.

On an early morning gym class during my freshman year of high school, I finally got my chance to get the old team back together. Just like in middle school, Howard, Jerry and I were all assigned to the same gym class, and just like in middle school, the frosty February mornings were tough to get through. Our gym teacher, Coach Thomas, was always in high gear and would dance around like a man on fire during those wintry mornings. We must have played every sport known to man during my freshman year. Football, baseball and basketball to start, and weird stuff too, like European sideline handball and a game Coach called "Crazy Ball," which was really some lunatic version of soccer with a ball the size of a mail truck.

That spring though, he managed to come up with a surprisingly normal idea that didn't involve being mauled by a soccer ball too big for wooly mammoths to play with. The Olympics were coming around that summer and in honor of the games, we spent the spring trying our hands at each of the track and field events. Once again I was reminded of Mark Anthony and that shiny gold medal. It had been a while since I had given that much thought, but each time we participated in an Olympic event I couldn't help but think about a gold medal hanging from my neck.

I was fourteen years old and hadn't given too much thought to what I wanted to be when I grew up. I did know a few things though: I didn't want to talk on the phone a lot, I didn't want to work in a factory or at a construction site and I wanted nothing to do with plumbing or electricity. I hated blood so I couldn't be a doctor, I didn't want to be a lawyer and was too shy to be a schoolteacher. Plus, I couldn't get a gold medal in any of those things.

I thought about basketball after I hit my growth spurt, but it had been over a year now since I'd grown at all, and I was pretty sure that this was my final height. As for other sports; well, I can't catch real well, so I can't play football. I can't serve, so tennis is out. My eyes are terrible, so I could never hit a curveball in baseball. I guess I always liked running, but I never really thought of it as being a sport. Spending so much time as a kid being chased home by Ike and whatever other goons he had at his side that day, running had always been a survival tactic. But when Coach Thomas told us that we'd be running relay races, I couldn't help getting excited. I mean, I wasn't ready to make a career of it, but my heart did beat extra fast when I thought about the pending race.

Coach Thomas lined us up, instructing us that teams of four would pass the wooden baton around the track for one lap each. All together there were enough guys for six teams. I sat back feeling pretty confident that I'd be among the first few picked. But then Coach Thomas threw a wrench into the plan. Picking the last two captains, he slowly worked his way over to my side of the pack.

"Okay, Mat, you're captain of team five and Dede, you take team six." Reluctantly holding out my hand to receive the baton, I watched Coach Thomas motor off hungrily to get the track set up, leaving us behind to pick teams on our own.

I glanced down the line at Howard and Jerry, who looked as if they couldn't wait for the torture of picking teams to be over with. I remembered when I used to be picked last right alongside them. I could see the pain in their faces and knew that today, I would have a chance to relieve some of it.

There I stood as the five other boys ahead of me made their selections, a responsibility I'd proven I couldn't handle, but had to in this situation. I flashed back to the last time I had to pick teams on a cold morning in gym class. I thought about the trouble I'd caused and the friends I'd lost because of it. "What are you waiting for, Dede. You're up. Pick twice because you're last," Mat (who I'd grown apart from since the night of the dance), snorted impatiently. The opportunity to make things right with Howard and Jerry was sitting right in front of me. The only question was whether I was brave enough to take it. I knew all the other boys in class would make fun of me for picking my old pals and I didn't know if I was strong enough to stand up to that kind of teasing. Still though, it was my chance to let them know that I wasn't the same jerk who'd been so mean to them.

"I'll take Howard and Jerry," I said, and the pack of restless boys went quiet.

"You're kidding, right?" scoffed Mat and a few others, thinking for sure I was playing a joke on the two nervous boys.

I shot a stare back at them, trying to hold my ground. The laughing really picked up when the crowd realized I was serious. Quickly, the teasing shifted from Howard and Jerry over to me. "Dede's lost his mind!" Todd Parker yelled. I could feel my resolve weakening. Then I thought about the way Mat treated me at the dance. I knew then, that beside Carla, Howard and Jerry were the only real friends I'd ever had. My strength returned and I snapped back at the circling crowd, "You guys worry about picking your own teams and we'll figure the rest of this out on the track." Still snickering, the crowd settled down, realizing the challenge I'd made.

Howard, Jerry and I made our way over to the track where Coach Thomas was just about ready with the fourth member of our team, Jamal, a new kid at school, who looked like a decent athlete. I tried to shoot the two of them a friendly smile as we walked, but they didn't trust me and thought for sure this was a plot to make them look bad. Finally Howard broke the awkward silence. "I don't know what you're up to, Dede, but if you think we're going to stand by while you humiliate us again, you've got another thing coming," he spoke angrily through a tight jaw.

"Yeah, if you made that challenge just to embarrass us, you're in for a big surprise, Savage," Jerry added harshly as the two of them tore off, taking their positions along the track.

The teams were set and we awaited the start from Coach Thomas. I was in the first position, followed by Jamal, then Jerry in third and Howard had the anchor leg. The anchor leg is usually reserved for the fastest one on your team and even though that was probably me, Howard placed himself there and Jerry took third. If they were going down, they were going down fighting.

I was ready to begin and looked up to see the two of them pacing back and forth in their lanes, both eyeing me down as Mat got in a few last minute jabs before the start. "You and the reject team have no chance, Savage," he bellowed. "See you at the finish line," he added sarcastically, but I ignored him. It didn't really matter to me if we won or lost. I was more concerned with mending friendships and getting the old team back together.

Coach Thomas ambled over to the starting line and called us to our marks in his best starter imitation. He then clapped two blocks of wood together, mimicking the firing of a pistol, and turned us loose. I got out pretty quickly but so did Mat. I was a few steps behind him and locked in a tight race for second with Daryl, the captain of the third team. I saw Jamal up ahead waving his arms, signaling to me that he was ready to take the baton. Then I put the jets on, reaching deep for speed that I didn't know my legs could produce. I think Mat was more surprised than I was when I flew past him in the final twenty yards. By the end of my leg we had sole possession of first place and I executed a decent pass to Jamal.

He stumbled out of the exchange and was no more graceful when he finally regained his balance. His arms swayed from side to side, his head bobbed up and down. He looked like he was towing a dog sled behind him and nearly tripped so many times I thought for sure there was no way he'd finish the race without a mouthful of track rubber. By the second half of his leg the "bear" was climbing all over him, which is to say he'd spent all his energy and could no longer run fast. When he reached Jerry, our team had fallen into last place.

They made the feeble baton exchange and Jamal collapsed in a heap as Jerry took off trailing behind five other teams. It was then that the miracle began to take shape. Exploding out of the baton exchange Jerry tore around the track, wide-eyed with saliva flying from his mouth each time he exhaled. He was frightening to watch, but most importantly, by halfway into his turn, he'd made up the fifteen-yard gap the leaders opened up on us during Jamal's leg. Jerrry had single-handedly put us back into contention.

It was a three-man race as Jerry approached Howard, having overtaken third place and now threatening for second. He passed the wooden baton to Howard and also passed through the same ferocity that drove his stretch. Immediately after the exchange Howard's thin body uncoiled powerfully, propelling him into sole possession of second place in only a matter of strides.

Howard and the anchor leg of Mat's team were neck and neck as they entered the final turn. It was the kind of comeback you only see in movies and everybody watching looked shocked. With the fiery intensity I saw in Howard's eyes, I knew there was only one way for the race to end. Mat's anchor tired noticeably and fell back nearly half a stride. Coming out of the final turn it looked like the "reject team," as Mat had dubbed us, was going to do it and make good on that foolhardy challenge I extended beforehand.

Howard was pulling away and with only about twenty meters to go it seemed he'd be able to hold on for sure. I was so excited that I almost didn't notice Mat inching his way toward the finish line. Knowing how much he hated to lose I was sure he was up to something. He stuck his leg into Howard's lane, hoping to trip him as he passed, taking away what would be an amazing moment. Howard was so focused on the finish line that he couldn't see anything else, and I knew that if I didn't stop Mat, Howard would end up tumbling onto the infield grass, humiliating himself. I bolted toward Mat with a full head of steam.

With Howard only a few steps from disaster, I reached Mat, tackling him to the ground before he could do any damage. Howard broke through the tape and was met by a rush of students and a beaming Coach Thomas, all congratulating him and Jerry on the miraculous comeback. I pushed Mat back to the ground and quickly went to join in the celebration.

The crowd dispersed and before long we were heading back in to shower. Howard and Jerry found me walking alone behind the rest of the class. Howard grumbled, "I saw what you did to Mat at the end of the race there. Thanks." I was so happy that he and Jerry were willing to talk to me again that I let out a sigh of relief and looked up at them smiling, but their stern faces quickly reminded me of all the trouble there was between the three of us.

"Do you think this makes up for all the mean stuff you did

to your two best friends?" Jerry asked. I shook my head.

"Just as long as you know it," Howard said, putting his hand on my shoulder and grinning. "You're all right, Savage." Jerry joined us and we walked back to the locker room as a team.

CHAPTER SIX

TIMING

Striding carefully along the infield grass on my way back to the starting line, I watched the line judge track down Enzo, the Italian competitor. He let him know that in accordance with Olympic rules, he was responsible for the false start and would be disqualified if it happened again. Enzo had tried to get a quick jump on the gun, anticipating when it would go off to give himself what he hoped would be enough of an edge to carry him through the rest of the race. The problem was that he'd guessed too early and his take-off triggered the rest of the runners trained to move at the first sound they heard.

The crew set up the hurdles again and the line judge was just about finished talking to Enzo when we gathered at the line for the restart. I didn't see how quickly Colin got out; I was trained not to look. But I couldn't help noticing that he'd already cleared his first hurdle when I knocked mine down as the false start signal sounded. In order to do that, he must've had one of his signature superhuman starts.

There wasn't any time to think about all that with the starter quickly gathering everyone together for the restart. Where there was an almost relaxed atmosphere before the first start, the restart seemed hurried. The starter, unemotional the first time around, had grown impatient as the runners slowly trickled back to the starting line.

I did a couple of quick stretches and tried to gather myself, but I couldn't keep the image of Colin getting out so far ahead of me from playing over and over in my head. There was nobody better at these mind games than Colin and I couldn't believe I'd let him unsettle me. Pacing back and forth, completely rattled, Matsu's voice came cutting through all the confusion in my head, "Looking good, champ," he smiled from his perch directly across from the third hurdle, the first key point in my race strategy. He knew Colin's head-spinning start threw me off. "A quick start is only one part of a race, Dede. Stay focused." His soothing voice calmed my thoughts. I'd almost forgotten that I wasn't alone in all of this and breathed a deep sigh.

Once again, the starter's tinny voice came over the speaker positioned behind the staring line, "runners, stand by your marks." And with that the restart had quickly begun, this time without distractions. There were no television cameras to capture introductions, no smiling girls to take your warm-up outfit, everything was rolling quickly toward the beginning of the race.

I backed into the starting blocks in the same sequence I had the first time, but not quite as deliberately, feeling the *starter's impatience grow with each passing second. I still tried to be careful with my suspect hamstring, but after going through that false start without any real problems, I felt a little more confident that everything was okay and that the muscle would hold up.*

Colin, on the other hand, took his time settling in and I knew immediately that this time around he was going to play the game. Busting out that near perfect start last time made him cocky. He wanted to mess with the rest of the competitors even more than he already had getting out the way he did. The two of us veterans went back and forth, getting our feet set, repositioning our fingers behind the line, each of us trying to get the starter's attention by delaying before he called us set. Messing around at the line like that can take you out of your game entirely, thinking too much about the start and forgetting the rest of the race can prove disastrous. Finally, Colin gave in to me and reluctantly came to a stop, holding his position. I followed an instant later.

The starter's robotic voice cut through the arena again, calling us set. Just as I suspected, his attention would be mine when he finally fired the pistol. He wouldn't hold me for long. While the others strained to hold their weight in the set position, I rose slowly, knowing he would fire the gun in only a fraction of a second.

Howard and Jerry had it timed perfectly. Their exhibition during Coach Thomas's salute to the Olympics came less than a week before tryouts for the spring track and field team. Word spread quickly and at lunch the very next day, Phil

Markham, the team's head coach, extended them a personal invitation to tryouts that upcoming Saturday. You should have seen their faces when he asked them. "Now I can't make you boys any promises about making the team, but if you can run like Coach Thomas says you can, I'm sure you'll make a fine addition to my new crop of sprinters." With that, Coach Markham turned and headed out of the overflowing cafeteria.

Now I'll admit I was a little disappointed that Coach Thomas forgot to mention me as part of the miracle comeback, since Coach Markham barely even noticed me at the table when he persuaded Howard and Jerry to try out. But I was happy enough to see my two pals finally getting some respect. And even though I thought my leg of the relay was pretty impressive too, I hadn't received a personal invitation to the open tryout. I'd have to settle for being pleased with myself this time around and give Howard and Jerry their due.

During the rest of the lunch period the two of them begged me to tryout alongside them. I didn't want to try out for the track and field team. I'd already decided that I would give baseball a shot. Besides, we were only freshman and making the team would be a tough assignment, especially without an invite. Still, after much discussion, I reluctantly agreed to attend the tryouts, but I insisted that I was going to watch and not participate.

Early that Saturday morning I found myself at school, walking across the infield grass to join the rest of the track and field hopefuls. Seeing all those people gathered there was awesome and I have to admit, I really wished Coach Markham had invited me too. There must have been one hundred people there, vying for a spot on one of the school's four teams. It was amazing being a small part of something so massive and even though I had pretty much made up my mind to try out for baseball in the spring, track was making a convincing argument to steal me away.

"All right, ladies and gentlemen, before we break into events and time trials, everyone give me two laps!" Coach Markham shouted holding a scarcely used bullhorn at his side. Howard and Jerry took off without a word, trying to keep in line with the rest of the pack and drawing as little attention as possible.

Suddenly, a voice shook me from nowhere, "What are you waiting for, son?" Coach Markham barked at me, still holding that bullhorn at his side. Frozen in fear, I stammered some, but couldn't find the words to actually speak. "Do you need a personal invitation?" he continued harshly and sarcastically, not giving me a chance to gather myself.

On the defensive, I smiled meekly and finally managed to sputter out, "I'm just here to watch, sir. You see, my two friends Howard and Jerry…"

"I know who they are," he growled cutting me off, "What does that have to do with you?" He had me backed in a corner, so I shrugged again. "Exactly!" He clapped his hands together and lit into me again, "there aren't any spectators on my team, only athletes. If you just came to watch, I suggest you wait for the season to begin so you can buy a ticket and sit in the stands with the rest of the fans." I started to walk away, but he wasn't finished yet, "But if you'd like to show me why you wore those shorts and running shoes this morning, just to watch Howard and Jerry, then get on that track, Savage, and give me two laps."

I had no time to wonder how Coach Markham knew my name or to feel embarrassed about wearing shorts and running shoes to tryouts when I told everyone I was just going to support Howard and Jerry. I was almost a full lap behind the rest of the pack when coach yelled one last time, "run Savage!" And I did, jumping to my feet with a smile on my face, chasing the pack from a lap behind.

I finished the warm-up laps with the rest of the group and stayed close to my two pals as they made their way onto the infield grass for stretching. We stood in line like a platoon of soldiers doing push-ups, sit-ups, jumping jacks and a whole bunch of stretches I'd never even heard of. In the middle of this workout I started to look around at all the other guys who'd attended the tryout. I was trying to assess the competition. To my surprise, I was really concerned with making the team. I guess I did want to be a part of this.

The whistle finally blew, signaling the end of the stretching. "Report to your stations," Coach Markham bellowed with the whistle still stuck in the side of his mouth. "Distance people, follow Raul on a two-mile around campus, weight people to the cages and get warmed up, jumpers to the shed, sprinters come with me and hurdlers to the north starting line with Coach Albert."

Howard and Jerry knew exactly where to go. I, on the other hand, stood there looking confused. Coach Markham growled at me again, "Haven't we been through this already, Savage?" I let out a nervous laugh. "Don't know where to go, do you?" he said.

I shrugged again as he studied my physique, crossing his arms and placing one hand on his chin, "are you fast?" he asked.

"Yeah, pretty fast."

"What about the sprints then, like your two buddies?"

I thought about it quickly, shaking my head. There were only a few spots on the team for each event and I wouldn't want to be in competition against Howard and Jerry. Coach Markham circled me, studying me further. A moment later he surmised that the distances were out. Without a large chest for lung volume I'd have no shot to be competitive in distance. And my skinny frame would keep me out of the weight events too.

"Let's see, not the sprints but you're sort of fast. And you don't have the body for the weights or the distance…" Coach Markham said, thinking out loud.

"Hey Coach! Is this all the hurdlers you can throw my way?" Coach Albert yelled over to us gruffly and Coach Markham's eyes lit up. In an instant I knew exactly what he was thinking and exactly where I was going.

"I've got one more victim for you right here!" Coach Markham yelled back fiendishly.

"Hurdles?" I said to Coach Markham.

"Hurdles, Savage. You've got those long spider legs and you even said yourself that you're sort of fast. It's a perfect fit," Coach Markham said. "Hurdlers don't need to be the fastest or the strongest. They just need to be smart and a little crazy." His devilish smile made me think he was keeping something from me.

"Coach Albert will teach you what you need to know." He started to laugh again, "and Savage, make sure he shows you how to fall without breaking your neck." His hearty laugh faded as he walked away.

Before I could catch my breath another frightening man was barking at me, picking up where Coach Markham left off. Coach Albert, a thin man whose shorts were tighter than my socks, spoke in a scratchy voice, "hurdlers over here, son!" A lump formed in my throat, eventually finding its way down into my stomach like a tumbling brick. How to fall without breaking my neck? I want to learn that first, I thought. I gulped, wondering what I'd gotten myself into.

Out of more than a hundred people trying out for the team, there were only seven of us that chose hurdles. As I stared down each of the lanes and the geometrical rows of wooden and steel hurdles, I understood why. It was intimidating enough from a distance but as I got closer and realized that each one was as high as my waist, I thought for sure this would be the end of me. I'd have a hard enough time climbing over those monsters with a rope and grappling hook – let alone trying to jump over them. I wondered if it was legal during a race to crawl under the hurdles. I was sure I'd have better luck this way.

The good news was that by choosing hurdles, or rather having hurdles chosen for me, I'd made the squad automatically for sheer lack of bodies. But I couldn't help thinking that the rest of the hundred kids knew something the seven of us didn't.

With the barriers set up in neat rows, the three upperclassmen eased into a slow jog, taking to the hurdles. I quickly realized that watching someone leap over hurdles on television and seeing it live were two entirely different experiences. On TV there is no real sense of the grace and power involved, from the initial attack to dragging that back leg through and landing right in stride. It was the first time I'd seen it and it gave me goose bumps.

I stood last in line, my mouth wide open, mesmerized by the other runners. So much so, that I didn't even notice when it was my turn. I was at the front of the line and all that was ahead of me was a line of hurdles. "We don't have all day here, Savage. Let's see what you've got." Coach Albert's voice woke me from my daze, but still I hesitated. I stared ahead of me at the enormous barriers and pictured myself collecting my broken teeth from the track rubber after collapsing face-first.

"Just run fast and don't jump too early. And don't forget to drag that back leg over the top or you'll really crash." He smiled. These were my instructions? There was no way I was going to tackle those hurdles. I didn't know what I was doing! I'd break my neck for sure, just like Coach Markham joked as he sent me off to join the hurdlers. "What d'ya say now, Savage? They're not getting any shorter. Do you want to make this team or don't you?" Coach Albert grumbled with his hands waiting on his hips, obviously losing patience with me. I could tell the rest of the group was growing restless as well, waiting for me to jump or get out of the way.

Finally, Curtis Duke, the team captain and the best hurdler in school with the letterman jacket to prove it, stomped his way toward me and spoke gruffly, "Look kid, if you want to be on my team then get to it and jump. You're wasting our time." He cracked his knuckles loudly and punched his hand. "I'm gonna count to three. You either jump over them, or I'll throw you over." He smiled and removed his sweatshirt, revealing muscles that were bigger than my entire body. "One," he counted, cracking his knuckles again. Curtis had left me with two unappealing options. One way or another I was going to have my neck broken. It was just a matter of how I wanted it done. "Two," he took a step toward me. I knew that I was nearing a very difficult choice. I could jump that crazy man's hurdle and land on my head, or stand there lame and have Curtis do it for me. "Three," he reached out to grab me, but I was off and running, unwittingly hurtling toward the first barrier.

I was so scared of falling that I ran faster than ever before. I could hear the wind in my ears and my feet barely touched the ground as I pranced through the air. The first hurdle got larger and larger as I approached it. Now at that point I knew it was a matter of going over this thing or crashing right into it, injuring myself for sure. I wondered how high I would need to jump. Would I have to pick my legs up? All these questions flooded my skull as the final question arose, how the heck do I get over this thing?

I chose to fly.

I'd never gone over a hurdle before and hadn't even been schooled in the proper technique, but somehow my body knew exactly what to do. I took the next six or seven with ease and when I came to a stop at the end of the track, everything was dead silent and everyone was staring at me. Later on Coach Albert would tell me that I was a natural. What he didn't know was that in many ways, I'd been a hurdler all my life, jumping over bushes, fences, lawn furniture and whatever else Ike chased me over on any particular day.

I landed right in stride on the backside of the final hurdle, touching down gently and gracefully. I turned back to face the small crowd, "was that okay?" I asked Coach Albert. For the first time today, he wasn't screaming at me. His voice was quiet and he wore a surprised expression on his face, "Yeah, um, yeah Savage, that was real okay." He was stuttering and mumbling.

Coach Matthews, his assistant, was standing directly to his right with wide eyes locked on me. As I made my way back to the end of the line I heard him speak to Coach Alberts, "Have you ever see anything like that, Coach?"

Coach Alberts was still staring at me with his whistle hanging from his open mouth, "Yeah, on TV."

I took my place among the rest of the hurdlers and finally felt, after being at tryouts for some time, like I belonged there. In fact, for the first time in my life I felt like I'd found my calling. This was what I was meant to do. I knew it the moment I cleared that first hurdle. I'd spent my childhood searching for something I was really good at. It took me fourteen years to narrow it down. I wasn't a basketball player or a baseball player, and I certainly wasn't a football player. I was a hurdler. I fell in love with the sport the moment I soared over that first barrier – "love at first flight."

CHAPTER SEVEN

HYPNOTIZED

Like a spring ready to uncoil, I waited, set to move on the first noise I heard. I was only up and set for a fraction of a second when the starter fired the pistol and released the eight frozen competitors. Everything came alive at once, the gun awakening my body into a feverish dance. My arms, legs and every muscle that was a part of me melted together into a running machine. I could feel the top two spikes on my shoes catch the ground and sink into the rose-colored rubber track, ready to propel my body toward the hurdles.

As an athlete you can tell you're in a good rhythm when everything seems effortless. That's exactly how I felt powering out of the blocks. It was almost like I heard the gun before it went off, or like time slowed down for me at the moment the shot rang out. If there was such a thing as the mystical perfect start Matsu always spoke about, I was sure I'd just experienced it.

I could feel the first hurdle drawing closer. I was dying to pick my head up and see how quickly Colin had gotten out, but I had to resist this temptation and stick to my game plan. After nearly snapping my hamstring the last time I got too confident, I was careful to stay in control of myself at the outset of the race. A stupid mistake here could end my last chance at gold before it even began.

With arms pumping and legs churning, I accelerated hard toward the first barrier. I looked up right on cue and the hurdle rushed toward me. I'd hit each of my marks coming out, so I would have no problem hitting my jump in stride. I was deep in the zone, my body running smoothly and effortlessly. Each step I took was perfect.

I touched down right on my mark after the first hurdle and pushed the ground away behind me with the toe of my spikes. Top speed came quickly. Bearing in on the second hurdle, my thoughts moved quickly as well. "Attack!" I thought, lunging for the obstacle. My body flattened out as I threw my lead leg up and over the hurdle. My right thigh pushed hard against my chest and my knee brushed my neck. Had I been any more aggressive I would have driven my knee right into the bottom of my chin and probably broken a few teeth in the process. That's the kind of intensity the hurdles demand of an athlete. At any moment the line separating success from disaster can easily be crossed.

My left leg pushed off the spongy surface and didn't follow my body until everything was in flight above the hurdle line. My knee neatly folded under my arms like a plane retracting its landing gear and I pulled it over the hurdle with my arms swinging out powerfully, then recoiling. I sailed over the second aluminum and plastic barrier, clearing it easily and feeling the wind rush past my cheeks, catapulting sweat from the corners of my contorted face.

But touching down on the backside of hurdle number two, I knew immediately I'd made my first mistake. I missed my landing mark by a solid two inches, having made my jump longer than it needed to be. Although the average spectator would never notice such a small miscalculation, "floating" could mean the end of the race for a hurdler. And although I gained two inches in sailing past my mark, in the end it meant two fewer inches I had to cram those three lightning quick steps into before the next hurdle.

A mistake like this could ruin me, so I straightened my running lean some and slowed down the slightest bit, preparing myself to "hook" the next hurdle. I knew running a perfect race was nearly impossible and adjustments like this needed to be made on the fly. Hooking was my only option if I wanted to stay in the race and avoid a painful crash.

To hook a hurdle is by no means easy, but being as tall as I am and with my increased tendency to float, it's a vital skill. Hooking the next hurdle meant attacking it normally at first, but rather than kicking my lead leg straight ahead of me during the takeoff, I'd have to kick it directly across my body and begin my flight sideways. My execution here would have to be perfect, as the third hurdle was a key moment for me. This was where I needed to find that next gear and make my first hard acceleration. I've always thought it was funny how fans watching the race think we go full speed the whole time.

The truth is, hurdlers speed up and slow down again and again at strategic points in the race. Having this game plan solidified is just as important as the physical stuff.

At the third hurdle, not only did I need to shift into the next gear, but I would finally have the chance to take a look around at the rest of the field. This would give me a better feel for how I would need to approach the rest of the race. Hooking the hurdle would actually help in doing this, since by the nature of the technique, I'd be facing the inside of the track as I began my flight. If all went well, I'd be able to get myself back in stride and also get a good look at everyone else – particularly Colin.

"Steady, Dede. Hold. Attack now! Leg up, kick inside! Turn, look left; snap down and across, pull the trail leg through now! Punch the arms! Lean!" I thought in rapid-fire terms and cleared the hurdle perfectly. I was back on my marks. I couldn't have executed the hook any cleaner, but there was still a problem. Once I was back in stride and hitting my marks again I got a clear look at everyone else. I thought I would have a slight lead, but looking around, it was the exact opposite. I was nearly a solid meter behind Colin who must have had the start of the century, getting out ahead of me. That was the bad news. But it got worse. Somehow, the Russian competitor Boris Krazets had found his way into second between Colin and me. There I was, sitting in third when I fully expected to be in first. I couldn't panic, though. This was just another problem I'd have to overcome for gold.

As I touched down on the backside of the third hurdle, it was time to really turn on the speed and shift into that next gear. I flew past Matsu, who was set up five rows back in the stands, parallel to the third hurdle. He screamed, "Now, now now!" I knew exactly what I had to do. My chin lowered instinctively and my chest expanded, filling with the oxygen I'd need to power into the next hurdle. My face tightened and I exhaled hard, releasing a pulse of energy that pushed me into the next gear. I was really moving now and that familiar lightheaded sensation took hold of me momentarily. Such an explosive burst of energy requires more oxygen than normal, so with that extra fuel feeding my legs, there was less air getting to my brain. Luckily, my legs knew exactly what to do with all that oxygen. They started pumping faster and faster.

In that one motion I closed the gap between myself and the leaders. I was well within striking distance. Now it was just a matter of staying close until the seventh hurdle when I'd make my next move and take the lead for good. I'd gotten back in a pretty good spot and gold was within my reach, but something still didn't feel right. When I took my look around (over the third hurdle), I only looked to the inside lanes and almost forgot entirely about the rest of the field. Taking the necessary gamble and looking off to my right, I noticed the problem. Right next to me in lane five was Tommy Johnston, the other American. He had latched onto my pace, matching me stride for stride.

Tommy was the great mimic, notorious for latching onto another athlete, hypnotizing him and letting him do all the work until the final hurdle when he'd break free. I'd have to shake Tommy before I could even start worrying about the edge Colin and Boris had on me.

In the summer before tenth grade things changed for me dramatically. Howard's Dad got a job in Chicago and before Jerry and I knew what had happened, we were helping our third wheel pack up his baseball card collection for the Windy City. We kept in touch with Howard over e-mail, but it was never the same. It's funny how life is constantly in motion and people are constantly changing. I guess I always thought that my life would change and that everybody else would stay the same. Boy was I wrong. In the past four years I'd lost my friends, gotten them back, and then lost one again. All the while, I'd gone from a total nerd, to a popular guy, to a track jock. Life had thrown me one surprise after another.

The next one came two weeks after Howard left for Chicago when I asked Jerry if he wanted to run a few laps around the track to get ready for the season. When his voice grew quiet and he made up some story about having to help his sister with her homework, I knew something was up. "Jerry, your sister's only two years old, she doesn't even go to school yet. How could she have homework?" I asked, exposing Jerry's poorly thought out lie.

It turns out that Jerry was quitting the track team to join the drama club and was afraid to tell me. We laughed later when he told me that his master plan was to fake a foot injury. He'd always wanted to be in show business and I was happy to see him going after his dream. I went to see him in school plays every month after that and he was always the lead. Who would have thought that a couple of nerds like us would have ended up being stars in school plays and on the track team?

Although everything was changing around me, my goals and aspirations were becoming clearer and clearer. My dream came into focus as well: I wanted to run in the Olympics someday and earn a gold medal. I was more in love with track and field now than ever before, and in my second year as a hurdler I was having unparalleled success, posting record times and shattering one personal best after another. But still, Coach Albert (although he praised me often), constantly warned me about the dangers of relying solely on my natural talent and neglecting the importance of race strategy. I half-listened to him, but the truth was, I firmly believed that if I just ran as hard and as fast as I could, no one would be able to run with me.

Summer ended and school began. I ran cross-country during fall track and trained indoors during the winter to prepare for spring track. So by the time I had celebrated my sixteenth birthday and was almost finished with my sophomore year in high school, I was in the best shape of my life. So I wasn't too worried when I faced Joseph Turner in the mile relay.

It was the final lap of the last race of the afternoon, and with so much more riding on this race than another personal victory, I was determined to come through. We were pitted against our cross-town rivals, Madison High, and were dead even in points going into the final event. Whoever took this race walked away with the whole meet.

I was in the middle of a career day, winning both my races earlier and picking up a new sophomore hurdles record on the way. That in mind, and with rumors circulating of watchful college scouts in the crowd, I petitioned Coach Albert to let me run the anchor leg in the mile relay, a race well outside my training. It took some effort, but I finally convinced him to jumble the lineup and give me a shot to impress the scouts.

Our small high school stadium was packed with spectators. And the old stands never looked better than when they were full. The set-up was perfect – the excited fans and two high school track stars coming together to compete in the final leg of the final race. This was a great opportunity to showcase what I was capable of and convince the scouts that I was too much to overlook. Earning a college scholarship would begin today, I thought.

I grabbed the baton for the final lap of the mile relay clinging to a slight edge. I felt confident that I'd have no problem shaking Joseph Turner, a solid runner, but one I'd beaten handily in two races earlier in the season. Joseph took the baton a few steps behind me and went for broke. He sprinted hard, making up my small lead in a matter of steps. If I had been more experienced, I would have used his exuberance to my advantage, forcing him to pass me on the outside lane as we entered the first turn. Making him run on the outside would have had him travelling further around the track than me, even if only four or five yards. In the end, this could've been the distance that determined my victory. However, I wasn't that skilled yet and ended up wasting my energy trying to stay far ahead of him. I was using my ignorant strategy of running as fast and hard as I could the entire time.

It wasn't long after making the junior varsity team as a freshman a year earlier that I was recognized as the best underclassman hurdler and promoted to varsity. This gave me tremendous confidence, but I didn't realize my knack for hurdles could only take me so far. I thought I knew everything, convinced my talent would bring me wherever I needed to go in track. But while I was concerning myself with how I looked going over the hurdles, making sure my flight was stylish and graceful, runners I'd beaten earlier in the season spent their time doing whatever it took to make themselves better. The vast difference between their tactics and the way I approached training hit me right between the eyes during that last lap against Joseph.

He was a hurdler like me, but wasn't graced with my long legs and athletic frame. He wasn't particularly quick either, but the edge he had over me that day was more than you could stuff into a body. Training hard since our last meeting, Joseph had developed a tight race strategy that he stuck to. Little did I know, but as Joseph and I entered the backstretch, matched stride for stride, he was patiently waiting to make his move.

I was stuck in his stride pattern, not knowing how to break free. I began to panic. Slowing down wasn't an option and trying to speed up was impossible. Joseph's savvy running had already sapped most of my energy from me. Coach Markham told us stories from when he competed in college about this same situation. He called it being "hypnotized" by another runner's rhythm. At that moment I wished I'd been a better student. I was sure he'd given us techniques to get out of this rhythm, but I was probably too busy perfecting my victory laps. With a season of hard work under his belt and a better grasp of strategy than me, Joseph knew exactly what to do when this happened and I was about to get my first lesson in track and field mind games.

He began breathing heavily, obviously laboring as we came out of the final turn. I relaxed, thinking, "I knew he'd never be able to keep up with me the whole time." His head bobbed back and forth, his steps grew heavier and he fell back some. He was giving all the classic signs that he'd hit a wall and no longer had the energy to continue. My eyes finally unlocked from his hypnotic strides and

I focused on his breathing. I managed to break myself free from his pace and could coast the rest of the way to a triumphant victory.

Feeling the pain of running in one more race than I should have that day, I gave in to the pleas of my tired and oxygen starved body. With victory seemingly in hand I slowed up as I came into the last twenty meters. It couldn't have been for more than a second that I lost sight of Joseph, but that was all he needed.

In an instant, his labored breathing quickened and his steps grew lighter; he was bearing in on me quickly and I was completely lost. He'd counted on me slowing up and showboating to the finish line. While we were locked in stride he lulled me into believing he was finished and fell behind gathering his energy for a final push. It was all the edge Joseph needed. He passed me like I wasn't even moving, tearing up the last ten meters and collecting victory on his way.

Dad had always said that when it rains it pours. On the quiet bus ride back to school, I felt the storm brewing. My cockiness had not only reared its head on the track, but made its way into the classroom as well. When we made our way back to the locker room I realized that my problems on the track were just a small corner of a bigger hole I'd been digging for myself that year at school. I started to stress out, remembering that mid-quarter exams were approaching and I had barely been paying attention in one of my classes.

Everything got worse the next morning. I walked out of Mr. Everett's math class holding a paper in my hand with a big red F written on it. I had failed my quiz. I gulped loudly, knowing the big exam was only a day away. Life had been going so well that I'd forgotten about my studies. My grade on the quiz told me that obviously I didn't know what was going on in that class. I started charging down the hallway, looking at all the red marks on the page. I was in a panic. I had three weeks of material to learn and one night to learn it.

Jerry met me at my locker and consoled me for my F. We set up a study session for later that night and I breathed a sigh of relief, staring at my friend, who had earned an A on his quiz. "Thanks Jerry," I muttered, keeping my nose in my paper as we turned the corner. I wasn't paying any attention to where I was going and, as per usual, crashed into Carla on her way to French class. Let me tell you this, making a good impression on a girl is much harder when you spill things on her and bump into her constantly!

Picking up the books I accidentally knocked from her hand, I smiled, trying to think of something charming to say, but settling for not knocking her to the ground again. So I stood there with a goofy grin on my face, with Jerry grinning right next to me. Carla broke the silence, "Hey guys, Trish and I are going to Yellow Basket for burgers and fries after school, if you want to come along?"

Do I want to come along? Is the sky blue? Is rain wet? Of course I wanted to come, but the test I was destined to fail was only twenty-four hours away. I needed every minute of that time to study. As I was deliberating Carla smiled. Once again, I was hypnotized, and in my mind, there was only one choice, "sure, we'd love to."

Jerry nudged me in the back and whispered, "What about the test?"

Carla started to walk away, "Okay, I'll meet you guys by my locker after school. See ya."

At once, Jerry and I spoke, "See ya, Carla."

She left and I looked at my disapproving friend and smiled, "What's the big deal, Jer? I'll study when I get home."

When we got to Yellow Burger, Carla and I sat next to one another and shared a burger and french fries. We talked about track, movies, her wanting to be a doctor, college, and nothing at all. All the while Jerry and Trish seemed to be hitting it off as well. This was a big surprise to me. I had never seen Jerry talk to girls before, but it turned out that Trish was in the drama club with him and they'd become friends.

After we polished off a milk shake Carla invited Jerry and I to her birthday party next week, she was turning sixteen. A smile came to my face as Carla stole a fry from my hand. Carla Romero is turning sixteen, I thought, remembering the boyfriend rule that her dad had made. I'd waited two years to ask her out on a real date and next week I'd be able to do just that.

When we left the restaurant Jerry nudged me again, "The test, Dede. We should start studying."

I patted Jerry on the back, taking hold of Carla's hand, "I'll walk Carla home first and then I'll meet you at your house. How hard can one math test be anyway?"

CHAPTER EIGHT

LATCHING ON

Tommy latched onto me hard. We were approaching the midway point of the race and the two of us were still a few meters out of the lead. Between each hurdle I took three long steps and traveled ten meters, a little over thirty feet. I'd cover that distance in about one second. Each hurdle is forty-two inches high, and from take-off to touchdown, it takes me less than two tenths of a second to clear the obstacle. I could rattle off figures for days, the point is that the one-hundred and ten-meter hurdle race is a quagmire of numbers and mathematics swirling around in precise calculations inside each competitor. To the average spectator though, it is thirteen seconds of running and jumping, nothing more.

I charged hard out of the third hurdle and stayed strong into hurdle four, hoping that my ferocious pace would take Tommy by surprise and break him from my pattern. But he still followed, stride for stride. The more I tried to shake him the harder he latched on. His rhythm had hypnotized me and I felt like I was not only carrying my weight, but his as well. Tommy's game plan was working and with each stride my muscles deflated a little more. It was as if he'd sprung a slow leak in me and sat by watching as I emptied.

Like a pair of synchronized swimmers we came up on the fourth hurdle, a perfect mirror image of one another. In a risky split-second change of plans I decided to forget about Tommy altogether, knowing how quickly he'd bleed me dry if I continued sparring with him. Regardless of who was at my side, there were still two very dangerous runners up ahead of me. My attention shifted.

Pulsing with newfound energy, and feeling like I'd given myself a second chance, I erased Tommy from my mind entirely. I started my flight over the fourth hurdle with a new take on the race. I pulled my right arm back, sweeping it close to my body as I cleared the barrier. When I stopped it right next to my hip, I was ready to fire it forward hard. Matsu and I worked on this technique endlessly. It was called the "short punch" and this was the perfect time to pull it from my bag of tricks. The punch would cause my left leg to clear the hurdle easier, throwing my body forward with a powerful surge. This would provide the extra speed I needed to quickly make up some of Colin's lead and put me back into gold contention.

Entering the punch phase of the technique, where I actually fire my right arm forward, my decision to forget about Tommy came back to bite me. I must have done too good of a job forgetting about him because as I fired my right arm forward completing the punch, WHAM, our arms collided in mid-air. My tactic of ignoring him as he latched onto me was a recipe for disaster and now that the collision had occurred, it was a matter of riding it out until we both touched down.

Luckily, I landed feet-first on the synthetic rubber surface of the track. But Tommy got the worst of the collision, crashing into his hurdle. And although he resumed the race, he was no longer a threat. Knowing how lucky I'd been to come out of the collision with only a slight stumble, I kept a cool head and righted myself quickly, avoiding the sweeping arms of Colin Beckham a few steps ahead of me. The collision fortunately unlocked Tommy and I, but it also cost me a few steps on the leaders. I exhaled hard and headed to the fifth hurdle with new determination.

If I was going to make a move, I'd have to take the race to the ground. Colin's technique over the hurdles was just too good to beat. My only chance was to turn this into an all out foot race. This was a gamble, but one I had to take. My plan was to touch down before Colin and Boris, not allowing myself to sail over the hurdle normally. The risk here was that by bringing my body down from the air early, my chances of hitting the hurdle with my leg on the follow through dramatically increased.

I cut my flight time nearly in half and my leg hit the ground hard, the track compressing under my feet with my knees straining from the impact. I just had to wait for the recoil from the track rubber to do its magic. Physics dictates that for every action there is an equal and opposite reaction. I was counting on exactly that opposite reaction to shoot me right back *into striking distance. It didn't take long for the track to push back hard against my feet and propel me to the sixth hurdle faster than normal. But this race doesn't give you anything for free. The extra speed I gained cost me some distance. Being further away from hurdle six than normal meant that I'd have to stretch when it came time to take flight again. Colin and Boris hit the sixth together and I was only slightly behind, having made up most of the distance with a burst of speed, compliments of Sir Isaac Newton.*

I actually touched down over the sixth hurdle before Colin and Boris, using the same technique I had over hurdle five. Again I landed hard, putting an unusual amount of strain on my leg muscles. By the time the two leaders landed, we were locked in a three-way tie with only four hurdles left.

My next move was set for the seventh hurdle where I'd need to find yet another gear to make a strong push for the finish. I was looking good, but the question remained whether I'd burned too much energy through the last two hurdles closing the gap. The race was more than half over, but the real test had only begun.

I sat nervous and sweating in Mr. Everett's classroom, waiting as the test paper slowly made its way back to me from the front row. My long legs barely fit beneath the child-sized desk. I fidgeted nervously, lifting the mini-desk up and down with my knees. The crinkling and crunching sound of the paper being passed back to me was giving me a headache as I stared up at the sulfur colored cement walls. Finally finding its way back to me, the test paper landed on my desk with a thump.

I swallowed hard and turned it over.

There were ten questions in all. I scanned the paper up and down looking for something, anything that looked familiar. The problems may as well have been written in Japanese because I didn't understand a thing on that page. I wanted to run away. I wanted to raise my hand and ask to be excused. I wanted to throw up.

I took my time writing my name at the top, making sure that I got at least one thing right. I struggled through the test, shifting uncomfortably in the seat that never seemed as small as it did that day and filling the sheet with a messy pile of meaningless scribble. Three mangled pencils and a doodle drawing of an Olympic stadium later, I reluctantly parted with my test. When the bell rang, Mr. Everett was standing over me. I handed him my paper without looking at him and walked out stealthily.

The weekend passed quickly and before I knew it I was stretching at Monday afternoon's track practice. I managed to dodge my parent's questions about the test all weekend, changing the subject anytime it came up. But I knew come Monday, Coach Markham's suspicions wouldn't be so easily eluded. He'd spoken to me several times about my slipping grades and promised to take action if I didn't get my act together on Everett's test. Prepared for the worst, I was the first one to practice that afternoon. I got changed quickly and was on the track before half the guys even made it to the locker room. Coach Markham immediately spotted me stretching off by myself. As he quickly made his way across the field, his usually cold and business-like demeanor was colder and more business-like.

"Everett's test results are in, Savage. What do you have to say for yourself?" I couldn't even muster a shrug, silently staring down at my spikes. Coach continued, "You've put me in a tight spot here, Dede, but you know team policy. Failing a math test is simply not okay. Why didn't you ask for help? You know Mr. Everett would have stayed after school with you." I didn't answer Coach, continuing to stare at my cleats, waiting for his speech to end. He wasn't finished and the worst had yet to come. "I'm sorry Dede, but until you can bring those grades up you're suspended from this team. Now head back to the locker room." And with that he walked away.

Suspended! The word rattled around in my head like a heavy steel ball. When I walked back home from school that day I was more upset than I ever had been in my life.

The next afternoon I found myself in Mr. Everett's classroom listening to my parents discuss how poor my grades had been since the beginning of track season. It was awful. "The good thing is that it's not too late," Mr. Everett reassured Mom. "There's still time to get Dede set up with a tutor. And if he shows me the kind of effort I know he's capable of, there's no reason why he can't turn this thing around and pass my course for the year."

I had a good feeling about Mr. Everett's plan and thought for sure he'd talk to Coach Markham and I'd be back on the team by the end of the week. I'd only be out of practice for a few days and shouldn't be too rusty for the upcoming championships.

But Dad had other ideas, "What do you think, Dede?"

he asked. "If all this works out, and you get your act together, you should be all set to rejoin the team next season."

Did he just say next season? Not knowing how to react, I lost it and blurted out right in the middle of Mr. Everett's room, "I can't miss the rest of the season. The team needs me. You can't keep me off the team!"

Dad put his foot down, "Dede, your responsibility in the classroom is your first priority. Now I know how important track is to you but – "

I stormed out before he finished his sentence. I knew I wasn't helping anything by lashing out at Dad, but I was so frustrated that I didn't know how else to react. I didn't want to face the consequences of my actions. I wanted to be mad at my parents, or Mr. Everett. But the truth was, the person I was most angry with was myself.

A week passed and I reluctantly accepted the terms that Mom and Dad set, despite how it pained me. And just as I suspected, the team fell apart in my absence. We were a group without a leader and it killed me to watch us stumble through the rest of the season because of my irresponsibility.

The first meeting with my tutor was a day away and even though I was nervous about meeting him, I hoped he was the key to getting me back on track for next season. So I put away the books for the night and busted out a few sets of push-ups and sit-ups before crawling under the covers. I just hoped this guy knows what he's doing, I thought as I closed my eyes and faded into dreamland.

Bursting into my room that Saturday morning and tossing aside the curtains while loudly singing, Mom woke me for my first session with the tutor. The bright light of morning poured in heavily through the bare windows, nearly drowning me. I fell out of bed and eventually found my way to my tutor's front door later that morning. I knocked and waited.

Jerry had been a tutor for English class last year, so I was pretty sure what to expect from my tutor when he opened the door – thick glasses, pocket protector, graphing calculator ready and roaring, and some type of collared shirt – probably brown and green. But when he opened the door with bright smiling eyes, pretty dark hair, and not a he at all, but Carla Romero herself, I had to rethink everything I knew about math tutors. Maybe this wouldn't be so bad after all. Carla smiled and told me that she was going to, "make me the best math student in Everett's class." Relieved, I walked in feeling that this arrangement was going to work out very well.

Yes, I was off the track team, but I knew right when my eyes met with Carla's that by the end of these tutoring sessions I would be a great math student. With her help, getting back on the team next season would be a breeze.

She was all business and we quickly got to work. Her quiet smile and friendly face made the feverish pace she set seem okay. I settled in comfortably as we steadily plowed through what seemed like an endless pile of numbers, equal signs and decimal points. The hours passed and we'd gone over so much that I thought for sure if we did any more there'd be no room left in my head for normal stuff like my name or how to put on a pair of pants. I got up to stretch my legs and without even thinking, I instinctively picked up a basketball from the floor and tried feebly to spin it on my finger.

"Dede," Carla called my name playfully, trying to get me back to the books.

"Oh, right," I said slowly returning to my seat. But I was spent and couldn't sit still anymore. I needed a break. Somehow not more than a few minutes later, I ended up with the basketball in my hands again and couldn't resist dribbling it annoyingly as Carla continued to work. With the basketball spinning on my finger she finally broke down and picked her head up from the books in front of her.

"Dede," she said again, a bit more seriously this time. But instead of calling me back to the desk she stole the ball out from under me and just as quickly had the ball up on her middle finger in a tight spin. With a fiery look in her eyes, she challenged me. "Since we're not going to get any more studying done today, why don't we take this outside on the court, track star." Her friendly demeanor disappeared and her usually quiet way turned aggressive. Not to say that I wasn't taken by her transformation, but I couldn't believe there was anything to it, considering what a sweetheart she was while we were studying. I figured we'd shoot around some and that'd be the end of it, but when we arrived on her driveway she checked the ball hard into my chest, "play to seven by ones, straight up. Your ball first, Savage." It was on.

I put the ball on the floor and dribbled back and forth some, looking for an opening. I didn't want to embarrass her, especially on her home court, but I didn't want to lose either. I faked left and she bit. Going hard right I closed in quickly on the goal and jumped, expecting an easy finger roll. I didn't even hear her footsteps as she tracked me down, but before I could get the ball on the glass, she'd already come through and swatted it into the bushes.

"Nice block," I said with a surprised look on my face.

She shot me a coy glance and quickly retrieved the ball, handing it to me gently. With a patronizing pat on the back she sent me back to the top of the key, "You're going to have to bring something better than that if you want to play on my court, track star."

The rest of the game didn't go much better for me and despite giving the same kind of effort I would against a guy, she was simply too much. When I played up on her, she blew right by me. When I gave her space she knocked down jump shots like Michael Jordan. I'd grab a rebound here and there, and when I did manage to get a shot off through her defense, it clanged off the rim or fell way short. I found myself in a tight spot, down six to one, game point and she had the ball.

I played her tough on that final play, shading her to the right, knowing she had a harder time driving left. I swatted at the ball as she brought it up. In a flash, she crossed over, blowing right by me left, well on her way toward an easy game winning lay up. She nearly juked me out of my shoes, but I recovered and made a desperate charge toward the goal, looking for the block. I got on her quickly and as she laid it up on the glass, I jumped up from behind her and pulled it right off the backboard. It was a great play and I could almost see myself on the SportsCenter highlight reel, coming down clutching the ball in both hands. Then I realized I was playing a girl six inches shorter than me and was losing six to one.

We both landed hard underneath the basket and rolled

into the grass with our legs hopelessly tangled together. We went sprawling to the ground, laughing uncontrollably. Her arms were caught underneath me and we sat there on the ground face to face, looking at each other for a few seconds and pushing each other playfully before we finally sat up. I wanted to go in for the second kiss of my life, but backed off, fearing rejection.

"You did really well today, Dede. You should be proud of yourself for working so hard." I thanked her and told her that I still had a lot of work to do if I wanted to get back on the team.

"I wouldn't be able to do any of this without you, Carla." I said smiling. She smiled back and brushed a few stubborn blades of grass out of my hair.

We sat there silently for a moment underneath the basket. She had a puzzled look on her face, like she wanted to say something. Finally she asked mumbling, "Do you have any dreams, Dede?" Not exactly understanding what she was asking I didn't say anything and just shrugged back at her. "I mean, what do you want to do?" I stayed quiet, but she continued, "it's like, I have all these huge dreams, but I always feel silly talking about them. Do you know what I'm saying?"

"I guess so," I shrugged again, too embarrassed to tell her that I knew exactly what she meant. I had dreams of running in the Olympics and winning a gold medal – that was why I was at her house, studying on a Saturday morning. But my dream seemed too unrealistic. If I told her, she'd definitely laugh at me. I couldn't even pass tenth grade math on my own, how was I supposed to make it to the Olympics? I didn't know what to say next.

Looking off into trees behind her house, she continued,

slowly at first, but gaining confidence as she continued talking, "I want to travel, Dede, and see all those places that we've only heard about. The world is such a big place. I can't imagine spending all my time in one small part of it. I could be a doctor in another country or a foreign correspondent or something, there's so many great things but I feel silly for having dreams that are so big and impractical."

"You think your dreams are big?" I spoke without thinking, then paused. Reluctantly, I continued. "I want to make it to the Olympics and win a gold medal one day. What do you think the chances of that ever happening are?" I put my head down quickly after I stopped talking, wishing I'd never said anything. I'd never shared that with anyone before and wanted to kick myself for blabbing it to her. But when I looked up, expecting her to be doubled over with laughter, I met instead the same smiling eyes and friendly face that greeted me at the door earlier that morning.

Her face lit up, "The Olympics, huh? Maybe I can meet you someday in Europe or Africa and watch you run for gold." She giggled excitedly, and things became clear for me for a moment. Even now I was on my way to the Olympics. From that day, that moment, I began treating everything I did as a step on my way toward my dream.

"I think that's enough studying for today," Carla sighed. I concurred.

Walking back into her house she told me very matter-of-factly, "You know, that last play was goaltending, so I really won, seven to one."

CHAPTER NINE

BACK ON TRACK

Hurdling toward the critical seventh like a pack of wild hyenas, the eight of us had to pay extra attention to our technique. Fatigue was quickly becoming a factor and with "the bear" climbing steadily up onto each of our backs, the slightest miscalculation could lead to disaster. I needed to strike the perfect balance between caution and aggression going into the last four hurdles. Certainly it was no time to back off, but without the kind of energy left to compensate for a mistake, I couldn't afford to take too many chances either.

My gamble over the sixth hurdle was risky, but entirely necessary. It put me right in the thick of a fierce battle for the lead. With the seventh hurdle rushing toward me steadily, and locked in a three-way tie for the lead, I hit my mark and took off cleanly. Colin and Boris ran hard on my left. The three of us knew what was at stake. There was no more time for games.

I pictured all the sportswriters who'd written me off writhing in their cushy press box seats. Dede Savage was tied for the lead with just thirty meters left! Mid-flight, I paused and allowed myself more time than usual to soar over that hurdle. I wanted to make sure I was in good position to shift gears for the last time and explode off the track when I touched down.

For some reason this was always a tricky hurdle for me. Earlier in my career the seventh would inevitably find a way to reach up and bite me. I've learned a lot since those days, taming hurdle seven in the process.

Soaring like I did would drop me behind Colin and Boris a bit when I finally landed, but I was confident it was a move I could afford. I waited anxiously to touch down on the backside of the hurdle before I could go ahead with my planned acceleration.

The spikes on the toe of my lead shoe caught the rubber track and dug in. My trail leg tucked up under my left arm in perfect form and my right arm flexed mightily at my side, waiting to complete the punch phase of my flight. It would only be another fraction of a second before I touched down fully and went tearing off at superhuman speed toward the tape.

My trail foot sank into the synthetic rubber and I began my acceleration. That's when I heard it. Wham! The noise a hurdle makes when it reaches up to bite a hurdler. Thwok, thwok, thwok! The echoing hollow sound of the plastic crossbar and steel tubing bouncing off the spongy track surface. I was sure it wasn't me, but that didn't mean I was out of danger. Two lanes away, the Canadian runner, Vander Parks, clipped the seventh hurdle trying to make a move. At any moment he could come crashing into my lane. We all heard Vander's mishap and were well aware of the potential for disaster. Acting simultaneously on instinct and years of training, the rest of the runners accelerated hard, doing whatever they could to avoid the careening, stumbling, Canadian runner.

With tragedy averted and Vander's slip safely in my rearview mirror, I fired my fist forward and accelerated hard toward the approaching eighth hurdle. Luckily, I had avoided a collision, but Colin and Boris did as well. I was still even with them and three hurdles remained.

Colin managed to break free from Boris, who didn't have anything left after sprinting away from Vander's collision. He fell back steadily. I set my sights on Colin alone as Boris struggled to right himself. He eventually settled down, but not until he had fallen behind both Colin and I. It was a two-man race for the finish.

Colin reached the eighth hurdle an instant before me. I began my flight early, hoping I could take advantage of the few inches I had on him in height. I needed to beat him to the backside of the hurdle and again take my race to the ground. I stretched hard, reaching for the hurdle and pulling my trail leg through powerfully. I touched down on the other side cleanly. Colin's flight took him past me, but the speed he lost touching down allowed me to make up that extra distance.

We jockeyed back and forth, the lead changing hands several times in those few short meters between hurdles eight and nine. Heading into the penultimate barrier, number nine of ten, there was no clear advantage. Both of us knew it would *come down to the ten-meter sprint to the tape with all the hurdles behind us. Twenty meters, one hurdle left, and on the other side – a mad dash for gold. Colin and I were locked in a classic battle. Both of us were tired, ragged, our mouths gaped wide open, our muscles starved for air. We couldn't keep this pace much longer, but neither of us could afford to slow down. We knew exactly what our bodies had left and exactly how much track lied ahead of us. If we'd calculated correctly, we'd be running at full speed through the tape.*

It was the race I'd hoped it would be. Dede Savage and Colin Beckham, neck and neck into the last two hurdles. He was an amazing athlete and I was proud to have my Olympic career tied in so closely with his. This time though, I wanted to take gold from my nemesis.

There were no more moves to be made and no more games to be played. We emptied our bag of tricks getting to this point. The only thing left to do was run.

After a few weeks of tutoring with Carla I had a much better understanding of mathematics and for the first time in my life, I had a girlfriend. She was the only girl I'd ever liked and as it turned out, she felt the same way about me. What was also good was that Jerry was dating Tricia, so the four of us went to the movies together or hung out at the mall almost every weekend. I remembered back to when Jerry and I were nerds. I pictured Jerry begging Ike not to give him another wedgie. I thought of Howard with his thick glasses, and how I always used to get my fork stuck in my braces. I had to laugh at how much things had changed.

Walking out of the last class of my sophomore year, math with Mr. Everett, I grabbed my final test from his desk and headed anxiously out into the hallway. Sifting impatiently through his comments, I finally arrived at the last page. Staring back at me from the bottom right corner was a B+ circled in bright red ink. Directly beneath it, Mr. Everett wrote, "Nice turnaround, Dede, the only thing left to do is run."

The next year when track tryouts rolled around everything was different. Carla had the highest grades in school and was hoping to become valedictorian after graduation next year. With her grades, she could pretty much choose from any college in the country. And me, I was a good student again, hyped for my junior year. I knew that this season was critical in terms of earning a scholarship to run track in college.

So I was understandably nervous stepping back onto the track the afternoon of tryouts. I felt like a rookie, and knew I would have to prove myself to Coach Markham and my teammates all over again. The first step was to make the team.

Coach Markham's practices hadn't gotten any lighter since I left, and trying to shake off a year's worth of rust, I did my best to keep up. I spent warm-ups refocusing myself and imagining a perfect run. After what seemed like only a few moments, the time came to break off into events and I rejoined the hurdlers.

When I approached the pack of guys, the comments started right away. "Is that Dede Savage? I thought you quit on us, Dede? Are you back for a full season this time?" The guys were relentless and I knew I'd deserved it. By failing math last year, I'd let the whole team down. I tried to keep my cool, ignoring them. I knew there was only one way to shut everyone up – run.

"Well look who finally decided to join us," Coach Albert's familiar voice boomed from behind me as I lay stretched out on the infield grass. I wondered whether he was happy to see me, or if my presence annoyed him.

"It's nice to see you again, Coach." I started in, but he cut me off curtly saying, "Don't think we're going to hand you anything on account of who you were, Savage. I hope Coach Markham explained to you that you'll have to earn your spot as a hurdler just like everyone else."

In my younger years I would have been intimidated by a warning like that and probably would have walked off the field right there. Little did Coach know that every day during the past year I ran at least three miles and did a hundred sit-ups and push-ups. I was ready. Plus, I was reading books and learning more about race strategy. I spoke confidently, "I apologize for last year, Coach. All I'm asking for is another chance." I continued stretching.

Coach Albert nodded his head at me and spoke to the group. "I'm going to make this real simple, gentlemen. There are ten hurdles and one hundred and ten meters between you and a spot on the varsity team. You come in under sixteen seconds and you're on my squad, you don't and you can find yourself a ride home. It's you against the clock. Now line up!" I took my place near the back of the line and watched the first few hopefuls come up short of Coach Albert's sixteen-second cutoff.

My turn came quickly and he called me set before I'd

even fully gotten into the blocks. Still, I obeyed his command and rose very deliberately. The gun sounded and I was off like a cannon. I'd beaten sixteen seconds many times in my career, but under much different circumstances. Quickly, I was up to full speed, remembering how great running this race made me feel. After half a year on the sidelines I'd fought my way back. I ran with a passion that Coach had never seen in me. A brick wall couldn't have stopped me, let alone some sixteen-second cut off. I charged through the finish line, eclipsing **fifteen** seconds handily. I'd arrived.

Coach Albert's stern face cracked as he clicked his stopwatch, "He's back!" Coach shouted enthusiastically, "Good to see you, Savage. Welcome home."

After a less than stellar season the year before, the team rebounded mightily during my junior year and I helped lead the charge. With renewed determination and focus, I quickly regained my old form and watched as one personal best after another fell. I tore through the competition that year and the commitment I made during my time away (to become a smarter and more skilled competitor), helped turn me into three times the hurdler I'd been when I left the team. The changes I made landed me a spot in the league championships and a rematch with Joseph Turner.

The two of us stood at the starting line, waiting for the starter to call us to our marks for the beginning of the final heat in the four-hundred meter hurdles. I breezed through the earlier rounds and came into the finals without really being tested. When the starter called us set I rose quickly, anxious to get started. The crack of the gun echoed through the stands, releasing the eight finalists. Joseph and I tore out furiously and quickly left the other six behind. It was a two-man race that afternoon and with the pace Joseph set, I was sure it was only a matter of time before he broke away entirely.

I did what I could to stay close, but he appeared to be too good that day. He ran flat out from start to finish, trying to break the record. I was out to run a solid race and not allow myself to be discouraged by his seemingly insurmountable lead. *"Keep chipping away, Dede, run your race."* In the middle of this thought I noticed something. There was still a considerable gap between us, but Joseph was slowing. I shifted gears and the distance continued shrinking.

Joseph had gotten uncharacteristically greedy that afternoon and in going after that league record, he couldn't keep up with the strenuous pace he set. The bear climbed all over him down the stretch and he had nothing left. He'd put beating the record ahead of winning the race and his mistake put me back in contention.

The lead grew smaller still and heading into the last few hurdles I was only a few meters behind, chasing down a very tired Joseph Turner. His steps grew labored and clumsy, his breathing heavy and erratic. Touching down on the backside of the last hurdle, we were dead even and the foot race to the tape began. Charging hard into the finish line, I began my lean a few feet out. My outstretched arms clipped the tape just a fraction ahead of Joseph, taking my place as league champion after an unbelievable comeback. I left that day with a giant trophy and a giant boost in confidence.

But still, after one year away from track and just two

full seasons on the team, I was hardly a big name in the high school track world. Missing that sophomore season really hurt my scholarship status. Automatically, scouts assumed that I was "damaged goods" because of my academic troubles during my sophomore season. And an average senior year, complicated by a high ankle sprain that sent me home for most of the first part of our season, cemented the stereotype that Dede Savage couldn't be counted on. Don't get me wrong, when I raced, I usually won. But to a scout, durability was a huge issue. Nobody wanted to waste a coveted scholarship on a guy that was plagued by academic and injury troubles throughout his high school career.

By March of my senior year, with my head spinning in a thousand directions, I somehow managed to squeak my way to the state championships, beating my best hurdles time ever in our final meet.

While the rest of the competitors from across the state showed up sporting gear from the school they'd be running for come fall, I was still carting around the same tattered old bag Coach Markham issued me during my freshman year of high school. Sometimes I wondered if anyone remembered my junior season when I set two school records and beat out Joseph Turner. None of that seemed to matter.

Although the state championships should have been a happy time for me, stretching before the races made me very sad. Track had been such a critical part of my life for so long, I couldn't imagine what I would do without it. But the harsh reality was that without a scholarship, this was most likely my last tournament as a competitive runner. I'd probably attend Murphy College come fall. This was the best academic school that I'd gotten into and they gave me a decent financial aide package. My dream of running in the Olympics was fading quickly. Even if I did manage to walk onto Murphy College's track team, I wouldn't have time to practice. I'd be working nearly full time to pay for college.

The final heat in the boy's high hurdles was set to begin in about twenty minutes. I found a quiet spot on the infield grass of the practice field and went through my stretching routine. It didn't seem like it should end this way. I'd been through so many tough times that I figured I just deserved to have things work out for me. Still, I knew that the best thing I could do now was tear out of the blocks and show the college scouts (that were undoubtedly sitting in the stands to check out some of the younger prospects), what a mistake they were making by passing me over.

Twenty minutes later, introductions were made and the starter called us to stand by our marks. "Gentlemen," the starter began, "this is the final race for the men's high hurdles. Please keep in mind that according to the rules you each receive only one false start and the penalty is immediate disqualification. Are there any questions?" We each nodded our heads nonchalantly, having heard those exact instructions at least one hundred times before. In high school track, just one false start is grounds for disqualification.

My heart pounded in my chest following the starter's command. I quickly got set up in my blocks and waited anxiously. My head was filled with delusions of running such a phenomenal race that afterward the scouts would come pouring onto the field, offering me full scholarships to whatever college I wanted. I came set with renewed determination. I would not let go of my dream without a fight.

A moment later I exploded off the line like a rocket, getting up to top speed faster than I ever had. With my arms pumping hard and my legs gliding smoothly over the track surface, I hit all my marks and leaned forward into the first hurdle. What a start!

The first shot of the gun came as I began my flight, but the dreaded second rang out when I landed. False start! I felt terrible for whoever that was and looked back at the rest of the field to seek out the culprit. But when I felt all eyes on me, I soon realized that the recall gun was fired because I left early. My legs deflated beneath me and I landed awkwardly on the backside of the first hurdle. I brought my hands up to my face in disbelief. My race was over before it started. No scouts rushed the track. There were no scholarship offers. My last chance came and went without me. I vacated my lane, escaping the humiliation of the track.

I've heard stories about athletes staying in the locker room for a while after their final competition, not wanting to take their uniforms off and admit that it was over. That didn't happen to me. I didn't want to remember track this way, so I showered quickly and made my way back into the stands where my parents were. I didn't want to accept the end.

When I arrived in the stands, through teary eyes and a labored smile, my mother hugged me without saying a word. Dad shook my hand heartily and pulled me close for a strong hug. They asked if I wanted to stay, but I just shook my head. With sadness overwhelming us, we made our way out of the stands and back to the parking lot.

Walking past the starting line on our way out, a little man came out of the shadows, heading toward the same exit we were. He sought me out, extending his hand, and calling me by name. "Tough break out there, Savage. You looked good all season though. And how's that ankle doing anyway?"

"It's better, thanks." I was perplexed by the strange man's consolation and smiled suspiciously. Extending his hand again, the stranger introduced himself to my parents, "Ken Matsu, head track and field coach at the University of Southern State. That's quite a boy you have there. I've been following his career since he was freshman. I'm sure you're both very proud."

Ken Matsu. I'd heard that name a hundred times over the past year and should have recognized him, but it wasn't until he introduced himself that it hit me. My parents beamed with pride and I reveled in his compliments.

"So where are you headed next year, Champ," he continued.

"I'm off to Murphy College in the fall."

"Where? I've never heard of their program." He tilted his head sideways.

"Oh, I'm not running track there." I stared at the ground.

Matsu was shocked, "Why not?" He was confused, assuming I would be somewhere on scholarship.

"I'll be working to pay for school, so I won't have time to run track." I explained the tough reality of my situation and nearly began to cry.

With widened eyes he asked quickly, "You mean you

haven't been offered a scholarship anywhere?"

I shrugged and shook my head, "No, sir."

With this, he started laughing, and for some reason, I did too. "I almost let you slip away, kid." I wasn't sure what he meant and just stared at him blankly. He continued, "I thought that Northern California offered you a ride."

I shook my head.

"I'll be darned. Well, this is your lucky day, Dede." He repeated himself, "Lucky day, Dede - that's a tongue twister." We laughed again. "What I mean to say is that, Dede Savage, it is my pleasure to invite you to the University of Southern State Track and Field Team on a full athletic scholarship."

A second later I was lifting my mother up in the air and my father was giving Matsu a full on hug. The words I was convinced would never come, finally did, and I excitedly accepted Matsu's offer right there in the parking lot.

I was back on track, one giant step closer to my dream.

CHAPTER TEN

KNOCKING ON THE DOOR

Colin and I charged into the ninth hurdle at full speed locked in a vicious battle for the lead. I'd been cutting my flight short and taking the race to the ground, counting on the spring of the track's rubber surface to propel me forward. Colin stayed strong, and with his impeccable technique over the hurdles, quickly erased any advantage I gained by landing first. Two strides ahead of the rest of the field, I pulled my leg through and rushed to touch down on the backside of the ninth hurdle. It was the last race of the games for each of us and the last race of a long career for Dede Savage. There was no excuse for leaving anything on that track.

I make a point of never looking at the hurdles I'm clearing. Two steps before I take flight I start looking for the next target. I actually end up taking each hurdle blindly, putting complete faith in my training. That faith can often spell the difference between gold and silver. A less experienced runner may have begun to panic with the final meters of the race quickly disappearing under his feet and a lead seemingly impossible to come by. But at thirty-one years old, I'd been here before. I stayed calm, prepared to make my move after the last hurdle, knowing I had a chance to take Colin in the final sprint.

Two steps away from the tenth hurdle, I instinctively raised my eyes, searching for the next one. But all that remained was a ten-meter dash and pearly white tape stretched tight across all eight lanes. I pushed off the ground to take flight for the final time, with Colin close at my side. My eyes were wide, staring at the finish line. I kicked my lead leg over, tucked my trail leg up tightly against my side and went soaring through the air, hovering exactly forty-two inches above the track surface. It was at that moment when I felt a pop.

A muscle never completely goes all at once. When it does tear, it'll continue to function for the moment. I thought for sure my hamstring would hold up and get me through the rest of the day, but putting all that extra pressure on it, cutting my flight short and catching the rebound of the track must have taken more out of me than I expected. There are few things more painful and unnerving than continuing to run on a tearing muscle as it shreds into a sinewy mess. I gritted my teeth and began a determined dash down the final ten meters, knowing the rapid deterioration into complete atrophy was not far away.

My focus turned to Colin. I was sure he'd be capitalizing on my misfortune, taking the opportunity to run away with gold. But somehow he didn't notice the trouble I was in and ended up making a tactical error that let me right back in the race. *We came over the tenth hurdle together, but with no strength left in my hamstring I couldn't pull myself down normally and floated clumsily over the final obstacle. Colin watched closely as I came over, my loose technique confusing him. He had no idea that my hamstring was hanging by no more than a thread and mistook my graceless flight for an attempt at the "rope a dope." Originally coined as a boxing term, the rope a dope is an attempt to lull your opponent into thinking you're in worse shape than you are so he'll drop his guard. Colin thought I slowed down over the tenth hurdle in preparation for a decisive push for the tape once I landed. The break in my rhythm confused him so much that he broke stride and stumbled, nearly losing it all together as he touched down.*

When Colin's stumble gave me nearly a stride length's lead with less than ten meters between me and the tape, I resolved to not let my last opportunity slip through my fingers. I leaned hard and continued lumbering toward the finish line with Colin gaining.

I touched down, and even though my left leg was on the brink, it continued to respond. I leaned heavily on my right side, hoping to relieve some of the stress from my burning hamstring. Bracing myself for the thousand knives of pain that would surely stab my throbbing thigh as I planted it on the track surface, I clenched my fists tightly. The pain was like nothing I'd ever experienced and everything in the world told me to give in. I heard the pulling and scraping inside the back of my leg begging me to stop, but speaking to me even louder was the muffled sound of Colin's footsteps chasing me down. I heard all these things and set my sights on the tape, hoping the final ten painful meters would pass by quickly. Surely the only thing holding my leg together now was the momentum of years spent chasing a dream.

Streaming across the finish line is an electronic beam, just like they use at horse and racecar tracks. This beam determines the winner in a close race. The stage was set for quite possibly the closest race in Olympic history and the beam stood watch, waiting to determine whose shoulder crossed first.

The lean for the finish line is a fine art and nobody had it down quite like Colin Beckham. My lean for the tape would be a tricky maneuver without the leg strength to stabilize myself. I had to stay upright because it's not the first part of the runner's body to cross the line that counts, but the shoulder. Colin's swan dive-like lean takes full advantage of this, getting his head and arms out of the way and throwing his shoulders forward. It was this swan dive that won him gold when we faced off in Paris.

Five steps. I resigned myself to the notion that my hamstring would have to tear right off the bone for me to stop pushing. The flashbulbs around the tape started popping and the noise from the crowd intensified, not with screaming and yelling, but a nervous murmur of anticipation. Photographers took aim at us with their lenses preparing for the finish. I planted my left leg squarely into the track surface and the muscle screamed, but held for the moment. It didn't give me much, but I was still standing. My lead, although shrinking steadily, was still intact.

Four steps left. My spikes dug in hard and I pushed the track away behind me. I flew forward on the wings of a pow-

erful stride. Like it had a mind of its own and could sense the weight of the moment, my right leg took control with the strength of both sides in the left's absence. Colin's steady gain ceased after that stride and my lead finally stabilized. I had maybe five or six inches on him. At best, this would translate into two hundredths of a second on the clock, hardly enough for me to relax. I was locked in a one-legged mêlée with one of the greatest runners of his time.

Three steps. My rubbery left leg stuck into the ground and I pushed hard but barely moved. It was like revving a car engine while it's in neutral. My body strained and worked but I didn't go anywhere, my momentum carrying me to my right side. Colin smelled blood in the water and started into his patented lean, gobbling up my lead, which was down to a negligible two inches. I begged for something from my empty leg, anything, but it had nothing to give. My stride was short and Colin continued to lean in hard.

Two steps. The failure of my left hamstring awakened a snarling monster in my right, propelling me forward with an unnatural fury. The lead stabilized again, but I hadn't gained back any of what Colin devoured. I was in bad shape. My body contorted into a feeble lean for the tape, favoring my right side.

Last step. My right leg was of no use to me and my dreams were at the whim of a feeble left hamstring that lay in shreds in the back of my leg. I planted my spikes very deliberately into the spongy track surface, preparing for the final move, and pushed hard against the ground. My hollow left leg began to crumble under my weight. Then, out of nowhere, the gears started to click and the fragile leg responded with enough of a drive to throw me into the path of the photo finish beam. There's really no way to explain why the muscle responded, with most of it sloshing around inertly inside my thigh. But whatever thread it was hanging by, provided enough push to get me through the tape. I went through standing up but quickly came up lame, eventually collapsing.

Medics rushed over to me while the horde of photographers followed Colin as he flew through the line in a glorious dive and started around the track in a victory lap.

The official results hadn't been tallied yet, but Colin's dive was a thing of beauty and I was pretty sure the photo finish would verify what everyone else already suspected.

A summer never passed more quickly than the one leading up to my freshman year at Southern State. Mom said that going to college would be a strange time, big changes always are. She was right. I said goodbye to my parents, and friends too, that summer. I helped Jerry pack for Los Angeles College, where he was going to study acting. I spoke to Howard, who was going into sports journalism at Chicago University. And when I gave Carla a hug goodbye and helped her onto a train bound for New York City, I wondered if I'd ever see her again. I was pretty upset about it for a while but finally decided to listen to Dad's advice, ignoring my broken heart. "If it's meant to be it will happen with or without your help." I trusted his words and moved forward.

My freshman year at Southern State didn't go exactly as I'd planned. I made some friends and classes were fine, but on the track, I just wasn't performing. Much of that had to do with Mike Stone, or "Stoney," as we called him. He was the other freshman high-hurdler given a scholarship that year, and with only one spot open for the U.S.S. high-hurdles, one of us had to switch events. After Stoney broke the school freshman high-hurdle record during our first meet of the year, Matsu informed me that I would be focusing on the longer events, like the mile relay and the quarter mile dash. He saw my disappointment, reassuring me about next season, when I'd get my chance to run my race, the 110 high-hurdles. Needless to say, that year didn't go exactly as I had planned.

It was hard being kept out of the race I loved, but I knew it was best for the team and tried to handle it gracefully. That didn't mean I couldn't try to convince Matsu that I belonged in the sprints any time I got the opportunity. In the final meet of the season against Milner State, that's exactly what I did.

After a toe injury to the captain, James Hill, and an emotional speech to Matsu, I was offered my first opportunity in college to run the race I fell in love with five years ago. I stood anxiously by my blocks, waiting for introductions to finish. I wasn't even hoping to win the race, just to prove to Matsu that I could compete in this event. The question was: could I pull out second or third place, and give us the points we needed to walk out with victory?

The starter called us into our blocks. Shaking my hands out in front of me, I looked up into the stands at my parents, who always sat together in the same row. I rose slowly as the starter called us set. I could feel every muscle in my body, every nerve, pulsate. I wasn't experienced enough to get the starter's attention, but I watched as some of the senior runners waited to rise to the set position. Blood coursed through my veins and my thoughts became singular. I was locked in, waiting in the set position for the gun to cut through the crowd's murmur. My excitement must have shown. After all, this was the 110 high-hurdles, the race I was born to run.

Our stadium was overflowing with fans that came out to see us host our archenemy. Milner State, despite being eliminated from championship contention early in the season, seemed to have our number and always played us tough. Decked from field level to the nosebleed sections in the traditional University of Southern State red and gold, the stadium shook in anticipation of the deciding race.

The crowd hushed and a slow clicking noise echoed loudly in my head. I could hear the inner workings of the starter's pistol, the gears slowly retracting the gun's hammer. I anticipated the sound and exploded off the line at the exact moment the shot rang out. I tore into each hurdle with a point to prove and a season's worth of frustration built up from not performing the way I knew I was capable of. I took all those pent up feelings and channeled them into my legs, establishing at once an insurmountable lead. I rushed through the finish line well ahead of the rest of the field and took another fifty meters to slow myself down.

Stoney managed to hold off two of Milner State's best and came in second, posting a pretty mean time himself, one that would have been good enough to win on any other day. We finished first and second, collecting eight points for the team and nailing down the victory. With a first place finish against a top school, I just hoped I'd made enough of a statement to get myself a chance at joining Stoney as a high-hurdles specialist. What I didn't realize was that I made a much bigger statement than that.

Stoney tracked me down on the sideline, out of breath with a look of smiling disbelief in his eyes. "I just couldn't catch you, Dede, that was really something. That's gotta be a record," he huffed and grabbed a drink from the table. I couldn't even begin to think about times and records. All I could say about the race at that point was that it felt fast and weird. Matsu told us that when we ran beyond our capabilities, it would feel totally strange to us. I was in the midst of that feeling.

The announcer's voice came over the loudspeaker as the official times were posted on the scoreboard, "Men's one hundred and ten meters high hurdles: first place, Dede Savage—13.44 seconds, a new University of Southern State school record."

It wasn't just Stoney's freshman record that I'd broken, but the whole University's. That was the fastest time ever posted by a U.S.S. hurdler! I was shocked. Waves of high fives and chants of "Dede" rained down as the whole team circled around me, hopping up and down in unison and passing me from one set of hands to another. Nothing was ever the same for me on the track after setting that record.

James Hill, our team captain, managed to extract me from the mob and take me aside, away from the dog pile that had formed. He grabbed me stiffly by the shoulders. "You realize what you've done, right, Dede?" His solemn face stared in at me and he continued before I could say anything. "You made the qualifying standard." I still looked confused. He shook me and laughed. "You'll be invited to try out for the Olympic team," his voice rose as he finished the sentence. Putting me in a headlock, he dragged me back over to the pile of celebrating athletes. "Olympic trials are in two weeks, freshman," James said tossing me back into the unruly mob.

The Olympic trials were held that year at Lincoln University, thousands of miles away from home, family and friends. But before I left, Matsu and I met at the stadium early every morning for some extra training. With only two short weeks to get me into high-hurdle race shape, I wouldn't have much time to forget the low hurdle technique.

The high and low hurdles are two very different races. Rarely can a person do well in both. The low hurdles require patience, strength and long strides, while the high hurdles demand quickness, speed, flexibility and fast steps. Under normal circumstances, it would probably take at least a month to change my running habits back into a pure high-hurdler's, but we didn't have a month.

The time passed quickly and I still felt a little uncomfortable heading out to Lincoln. I sat stretching on the infield grass, hoping my instincts were still intact and that a season out of practice hadn't done too much damage. The meet was televised and every sportswriter covering the event was curious about the skinny freshman that no one had heard of. I had a good first run and finished third in the semifinal. To my surprise, this was good enough for a spot in the finals.

When the qualifying race arrived I was poised and ready. I placed my blocks firmly on the track surface and when the starter called us to our marks, I was completely loose, determined to have fun. After all, I wasn't even supposed to be here. It wasn't the race I'd run all season and I hadn't even dreamed of making an Olympic team until four years later. At eighteen, I was two years younger than anyone else in the field. I was a boy running alongside men. So my attitude was simple: *run hard, whatever happens, happens.*

I positioned my feet snugly against the pedals and dug in, ready to tear out of the blocks. My face twisted into a snarl and waited for the starter to call us set. The rest of the field took their time digging in. I was fortunate enough to have drawn lane three. The race favorite and America's best hope for a gold medal that year, Renaldo Swift, was to my right in lane four. In lane five next to him was Tony Foster, an aging veteran. He dug in trying to make his third consecutive Olympic team. I was honored to be lined up in the same field as these athletes and although winning was the first thought in my mind, I was also concerned with staying close enough to learn something. I studied Renaldo, copying his every move, right down to the smallest movements of his fingers as he positioned them behind the line. The remaining runners settled in and the starter called us set.

I came up quickly, knowing that with so much talent in the field, the starter would have no patience for me jockeying with the pros for the mental edge. Renaldo and Tony took their time. The two of them finally froze at the top of their crouch and the starter released us immediately, his attention focused entirely on them. The gun fired and they were off like nothing I'd ever seen before. They set a mean pace, but I got out cleanly as well and sat unsteadily in third behind Renaldo and Tony going into the first hurdle.

I pushed to catch up to Renaldo, but at the fourth hurdle he made his move, accelerating hard and pulling away from the field. Tony and I followed suit and sped up before he got away. I didn't realize it at the time, but I was getting a good lesson in how to latch on. I watched Tony's technique over the fifth and sixth hurdles and my legs instinctively copied his every move.

With my legs motoring beneath me and my upper body struggling to keep up, I stayed locked at Tony's hip, the two of us chasing down Renaldo who led by no more than a stride's length. Coming down on the backside of the tenth hurdle, Renaldo's lead was too much and he strode through the tape gracefully with one finger raised. The first three positions would make the team. Tony and I came down locked in a battle for second, but I wasn't sure of anything at that point. There could just as easily have been someone hidden on the other side of Tony who I'd failed to notice. Three steps to the dash for the tape and Tony pulled away from me, refusing to let some no-name college freshman beat him to the line. There was nothing I could do about it. I was spent.

Tony cruised in behind Renaldo, securing second place and a spot on his third and final Olympic team. As he passed by though, I got a clear look at all the space to his right and found myself staring at three empty lanes. The mystery man I imagined on the other side of Tony turned out to be an invention of my mind. I ran through the line, earning a third place finish and a spot on the United States Olympic Track and Field Team!

I crossed the line with my arms outstretched wide and my

face to the sky. Photographers took pictures of me and the next day the papers were asking "who is Dede Savage?"

There was no mob at the finish line this time and I didn't have a victory lap in me. I crouched down and buried my face in my hands. I wasn't even supposed to be here, but I was going to the Olympics, knocking on the door to my golden dreams.

CHAPTER ELEVEN

THE HIGHEST STAND

The Games rolled around quickly after the trials that year, leaving me with very little time to train. They took place in Tokyo, Japan and I couldn't have been more excited. I got there a few days early and traveled all over the country. I don't think I ever had so much fun. Maybe too much. I'd made it to the Olympics and had no idea how good the competition was going to be. Everyone I ran against was the best of the best in their country. They were all superstar athletes, some with Olympic experience, some without. But like me, everyone shared the same dream. The problem was, it would only come true for one of us.

I was still a low-hurdler heading into those games and I was simply outmatched, outrun and outclassed, making a disappointingly early exit from my first Olympics.

The four years between that first appearance and my second Olympic adventure were painfully long and afforded me plenty of time to think things over. I finished college, and graduated with honors. I filled much of my time between games putting together a pretty successful career as a hurdler, running in both collegiate and professional venues. Everything was great, but still, dreams of gold haunted me every time I closed my eyes.

I went into the Games in Paris, France, prepared for victory. In my prime, at twenty-three years of age, I was heavily favored to win it all that year. With an unparalleled training regimen and an early round loss four years earlier to make up for, I thought I was a sure thing. But even though I breezed into the finals, I still found myself standing in disbelief at the finish line, watching a young British runner by the name of Colin Beckham breeze past me on his way to gold. As good as I was that day, someone was better. In fact, three people were better. I ran a great race, but finished fourth, barely out of medal contention.

I ran the best race I could that night and left the stadium realizing exactly how special a medal was. Sometimes even the greatest of athletes walk away without gold. That was something I was having trouble coming to grips with. I had to get back – I needed one more shot.

What I didn't realize was that it would take me eight more years to get there. I went out for my third games at the age of 27 and broke my ankle during trials, missing what most people thought was my last chance at gold. Despite four years of training, I was forced to stay home while my peers chased their dreams in Canada.

Everyone said that Dede Savage would never step foot on an Olympics track again. Matsu and I weren't so sure. He focused me and had me training every day for four more grueling years. And at 31 years of age, I made the US Olympic team one last time, as the senior member of the team. I was clinging to the hope that my old legs had enough in them for one last race...

All that brings me right back to where I am now, collapsed in an awkward pile of myself, clutching a deflated left leg and waiting for the monitor to replay the end of my final race. I chase away the medics that are tending to me and, hobbling to my feet, fix my gaze on the blank screen positioned high above the stadium floor. Colin, now halfway through his victory lap and still being hounded by photographers, stops to look up at the now flickering display in anticipation of the slow motion replay. My already rubbery legs shake even more uncontrollably beneath me and it takes everything I have to remain standing. I'm determined to stay upright for the replay, and take the news, whatever it is, standing up.

The flickering screen stabilizes and the image of Colin and I coming over the last hurdle together materializes. The crowd waits in a nervous hush as the screen recounts, moment by moment, the final dash for the tape. It's all there. My left leg collapses after each stride and Colin quickly gobbles up the marginal lead I'd opened. Three steps out, he starts his mighty lean, in stark contrast to my own inept and fairly upright push for the tape. The camera angle shifts quickly to the finish line, a straight shot right across the tape – the perfect vantage point to determine a winner. Colin and I enter from the left in super slow motion, Colin in full lean, practically parallel to the track surface.

My eyes, dried out from not blinking, remain locked on the monitor as the angle changes again and the camera pulls in tight on the two of us from the chest up. My legs quiver and begin to leave me as the finish unfolds the way I had secretly suspected. His lean was too much for me, and my feeble bend for the tape just wasn't enough. The monitor broadcasts in full beaming color for the entire stadium, Colin's head crossing the line in an all out dive for the gold. The replay slows even more to show greater detail and even though it kills me to watch, my gaze is fixed. With Colin's head clear of the finish line it'll only be a matter of moments before he drags his shoulders through and makes it official.

In the picture, I lag slightly behind but something's starting to happen. Colin's shoulder is slow coming through. With such an exaggerated lean, practically horizontal, he put more distance between his head and shoulders than I did finishing upright. Colin disappears from the shot, eclipsed by my hard charging upper body. His shoulders eventually pull through the finish line, but not before I come stumbling across, stealing gold right out from underneath him and putting a shock into the crowd.

The sleeping monster coiled in the stadium awakens all at once. One-hundred-and-fifty-thousand heads erupting in a spontaneous and unified roar, shaking the stadium down to its concrete insides. There's nothing like it. My head spins. My phantom legs disintegrate beneath me. Now the photographers are running toward *me*, Dede Savage! Piled up on the rubber surface, my face buried deeply in my hands, I bend over and plant a gentle kiss in between the white lines of lane four. Pounding my fist hard on that now sacred track, I reach my hands up toward the sky, letting slip a deep and soulful cry. There are no words, no thoughts – only feelings. The weight of so many years spent chasing down a dream has been lifted.

I try to look up into the stands through the barrage of

flashbulbs, but I can't find my family. Cutting through the photographers, a heated rival reaches out his hand. Colin Beckham, my opponent just a few minutes ago, grabs my hand in congratulations and drags me out of the camera-toting mob toward the sideline. "It was a fine race, Savage," he says with my arm slung over his shoulder, helping me to walk.

My eyes, clouded by the flashbulbs, finally clear. Through the haze my family appears in the first row above the track surface. I am greeted by my mother's tear streaked face, my father's strained expression as he chokes back tears of his own and the same bright smiling eyes my wife has been looking at me with since she tutored me in high school. I kiss her gently. Dad was right, Carla and I were meant to be. We married right after college and haven't been apart since.

Ten minutes later I am fully dressed in my USA uniform. Out of the small opening at the end of the dark awards tunnel the three medalists slowly emerge into the dizzying lights and swirling roars of the monstrous crowd. At the end of the long procession of presenting dignitaries and costumed award presenters I feel tiny, dwarfed by both the crowd and the moment. The stadium seems strange and new. I can barely make out the track beneath the colorfully decorated floor. The familiar faces in the crowd are replaced now with a hazy whirlwind of flashbulbs and cheering fans. The moment unfolds before me. I walk toward the podium, three large wooden boxes, one higher than the other two. I climb up to the highest stand and can remember a million dreams of standing in this very spot. The reality outdoes them all.

Colin Beckham is on my right in the silver medal position and the very young Hans Joyce of Germany, just at the beginning of his career, stands proudly in third. The flashbulbs subside momentarily in anticipation of the ceremony. The crowd digs in, and looking up, I see Matsu standing solemnly, holding one finger up on his raised hand. My parents and Carla sit in front of him locked in a soft embrace. My father fights back tears, but they grow too much for him. And finally, my two old pals, Howard and Jerry, their arms wrapped around the shoulders of their wives, give me smiling nods of approval. I'm sure none of them can see me do it, but I mouth the words, "Thank you," and smile back.

The announcers open the men's 110-meter high hurdle medal ceremony. Hundreds of white doves are released into the clear blue sky. The Olympic flame burns brightly and the flags unfurl. I bow my head. The gold medal I had dreamt about for most of my life is placed over my head and now hangs upon my neck. It is everything I thought it would be. The national anthem plays loudly as I stand alone atop the highest stand, above and on top of the world.

TEST YOURSELF...ARE YOU A PROFESSIONAL READER?

Chapter 1: Showing Up

Who is Colin Beckham? Explain.

Why did Howard and Jerry retire from backyard football?

Who is Ike "Spike" Gwynn? Would you say that he's a friendly competitor in a game of touch football? Explain.

ESSAY

In this chapter, Dede was constantly razzed and picked on by Ike and Tony. How did this make him feel? How would you feel if you were the victim of such verbal and physical abuse?

Chapter 2: Standing Up

Why was Dede satisfied to have drawn "lane four" as his running lane in the Olympic race?

Dede could always tell how fast he was running because of one sound in particular. What was that sound?

According to Dede, what was even "cooler" than the fact that he stood up to the bullies?

ESSAY

Michael Anthony and his words convinced Dede to stand up for himself. Michael said that "you need the courage to stand up to people who try and tell you what you can't do." How could those words help you in your daily life?

Chapter 3: Stumbling

What weakness did Dede see in the young runners as they immediately fled to the temporary track for some last-minute practice?

What were some of the consequences of Dede's sticking up for himself in front of Ike?

Was Carla, Dede's dream girl, impressed with the changed manner in which Dede treated Howard and Jerry? Explain.

ESSAY

When Dede's "two worlds" and two circles of friends collided before a pick-up basketball game, he was left to choose between Howard and Jerry and his "new friends." Who did he choose and why? When he had a chance to reflect upon his actions, was he proud or ashamed of himself? Explain.

Chapter 4: Out of the Darkness

What was the result of Dede's mistake during one of his warm-up runs?

How did Allen bully Dede?

How does Dede feel when he is not chosen for Mat's trip to the amusement park?

ESSAY

In this chapter, as Dede chases down Brenda's mom's car, he realizes that he possesses a special talent—he can run like the wind blows. Describe a unique talent that you have. When did you first realize this talent? How often do you practice your talent?

Chapter 5: Taming the First Hurdle

What was Dede's main concern and the last item on his "checklist" as he entered the starting blocks for his final race?

How important was Dede's first step in the overall scheme of the race? Explain.

Though Dede hadn't spent much time thinking about his future, he knew (with certainty) that he eventually didn't want to do a few things. Name those careers.

ESSAY

Dede selects Howard and Jerry to his track team in Chapter 5. Why did he do this? What were Howard and Jerry's initial reactions to these shocking choices? Would you have forgiven Dede?

Chapter 6: Timing

In an Olympic race, what happens to a runner when he or she false starts for a second time?

Why was Dede intrigued and pondering a tryout of his own when he showed up to watch Howard and Jerry compete for spots on the track team?

Name a pair of reasons that Coach Markham sent Dede to run hurdles when Dede didn't know which event to try out for.

ESSAY

Coach Markham and Coach Albert encourage Dede with their words in this chapter. He adheres to their prodding and decides to run. Who is the person in your life that encourages you with their words? What has their belief meant to you?

Chapter 7: Hypnotized

Why was the third hurdle so important to Dede and his race strategy?

What was the "true" reason for Jerry wanting to quit the track team? What did he plan to use as his "fake" excuse for leaving the team?

Why was Dede so excited that Carla was about to turn sixteen years old?

ESSAY

"Life had been going so well that I'd forgotten about my studies," Dede says in this chapter. Due to this neglect, Dede fails a math quiz and loses his grip on his schoolwork. Name a time in your life when you were distracted from your studies and detail why your grades suffered. What did you learn from this experience?

Chapter 8: Latching On

To whom did Dede shift his attention as he approached the fourth hurdle?

Why was Dede fidgeting nervously in his seat during the big test in Mr. Everett's math class?

When Dede arrived at his tutor's house, why was he suddenly convinced that he was going to become a great math student?

ESSAY

In this chapter, Dede and Carla have a long talk about dreams and both of them confess their personal dreams to each other. What is your dream? What obstacles stand between you and your dream? How will you overcome these obstacles?

Chapter 9: Back on Track

Why was Dede nervous when he heard Vander Parks's hurdle snap?

How did Dede react to Coach Markham's hazing when he rejoined the team? How would he have reacted to such treatment when he was younger?

Why did Dede feel a sense of sadness when he stretched before his final race in high school?

ESSAY

In Chapter 9, we read that Dede's hard work and practice with his math pays huge dividends. Detail how his improved grades positively affected his track career. What did his turnaround teach you?

Chapter 10: Knocking on the Door

Describe Colin Beckham's unique finishing move at the conclusion of a race.

According to Matsu, why did Dede feel strange during his first college victory?

What skills are required to run a race with low hurdles? High hurdles?

ESSAY

In his final race, Dede took his body and his hamstring beyond the limit of pain that he thought was humanly possible. Though his body tried to convince him to give in and give up, Dede simply refused to quit. Name a time in your life when you didn't think your body or your mind could go any further, yet you didn't quit. What did you learn about yourself because of this experience?

Chapter 11: The Highest Stand

How did Dede fare in his first Olympic Games?

Was Dede satisfied with the race that he ran during the Olympics in Paris? Explain.

What is "The Highest Stand?"

ESSAY

Congratulations! You have completed a Scobre Press book! After joining Dede on his journey, detail what you learned from his life and experiences. What did Dede teach you about what character traits you will need to overcome "hurdles" in your daily life?